THE MARINE IN UNIT A

A Gay College Romance

LEE SWIFT

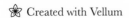 Created with Vellum

Acknowledgments

This is dedicated to my niece, Kelsi Hakala. She and I share a love of the written word. I am so proud of the works she is producing in poetry. She is an amazing poet.

Thank you for allowing me to include your poem in the book, Kelsi. It truly captured the emotion that Oliver was feeling when he was just a teenage boy.

Mockingbird Place

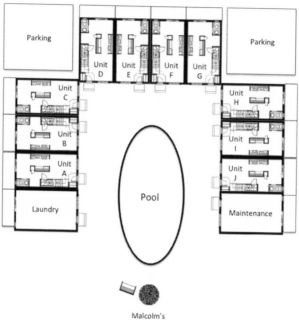

Malcolm's
Tree

Chapter 1

E ven though the sun is shining and there isn't a cloud in sight, darkness threatens to suffocate me. I hold the urn tightly, concerned that I might drop it since my hands are shaking. It contains the ashes of the man who rescued me six years ago when I was only fifteen.

Malcolm Rivers.

How am I to survive without him? I have no clue. God, I'm not ready to say goodbye.

I stand next to Candy and twelve of my neighbors, though they are more than just neighbors to me. They are my family, like Malcolm and Candy. And he was family to them, as he was to me. I'll never forget his definition of family. "Blood isn't thicker than water, Oliver. Love is. That's what makes a real family."

Along with being a friend, a mentor, someone I looked up to, he was like my dad, much more than my biological father has ever been, though in truth Malcolm was old enough to be my grandfather.

Was. What a terrible word to associate with a person. So final. So permanent. So awful.

This memorial ceremony in our courtyard next to the pool is to honor one of his last requests. Most would find the 12-unit, U-shaped, Mediterranean complex where we live a poor excuse to hold such a solemn observance, but not us. Sure, it could use a fresh coat of paint and the rain gutter above the laundry room could be tightened. But Mockingbird Place is special, unique, and warm. And on this day it's a very sacred space. It is *his* home and ours.

"Oliver, it's your turn." Martha is Malcolm's cousin and lives in Unit I with her partner Sarah.

"Give me a second." I try to compose myself but can't. I'm a wreck.

"Take all the time you need, sweetie," Sarah tells me.

Now that Malcolm is gone, Martha, Sarah, and I are the new owners of Mockingbird Place. He left it to us. Since I'm still in college, Martha and Sarah will manage the complex for us until I graduate. At seventy-two, both are as young at heart as Malcolm ever was.

They have been together for decades and want to get married. They could have already gone to one of the states where same-sex marriage is legal, but they want to be married in our courtyard surrounded by us, their friends. Their family.

The Supreme Court will rule on marriage equality this week or next. God, I wish Malcolm could have been here when the decision comes down. He was so excited about the case before the court. He believed they would rule in our favor and same-sex couples would have the right to marry in all the states, including ours—conservative Texas. I'm cautiously optimistic. We're going to have a barbeque Friday just in case the decision comes down and we have something to celebrate. Even if it doesn't and we have to wait until next week to find out, we're still going to get together. We always have fun when we do.

But will we still? Without Malcolm? I don't know if I can.

His will, which isn't written in typical legalese, says all that needs to be said about us, including Martha and Sarah. *They are the biggest ducks in the puddle at pool parties. And what can I say about my dear boy Oliver. He's very special to me and I know he's going to succeed in whatever he pursues. I want him to be happy. Martha, Sarah, and Oliver will take great care of Mockingbird Place for me. I couldn't leave my home in better hands.*

I stare at his Rolex he also left me.

On paper, my friendship with Malcolm doesn't make sense. He and I are from very different backgrounds. He was born nearly sixty years before my birth. He came from a Catholic home with nine siblings in Philadelphia. I'm from small town Winters, Texas. I grew up in my parents' hell-fire-and-damnation Baptist church. And I don't have any siblings. I'm an only child.

But despite all that, Malcolm and I have a connection, deep and unbreakable, that comes from both our hearts. Not *comes. Came.* Damn those words.

This is the last of several memorial services for Malcolm, though there is nothing religious about this one or the earlier services. His month-long send-off began with a dinner party the night after his death followed by many festive gatherings at all the clubs on Cedar Springs. Over five hundred of his friends from around the country attended last night's affair. He was a man who had quite an impact on many people during his life. Today's much smaller ceremony, once again ordered by Malcolm, is for the thirteen of us, the current residents of Mockingbird Place.

"You need each other, my darlings, now more than ever. I wish I could have lived longer, but my work here is done. You are my last family, my last legacy. Be happy, that's all I ask."

The paperwork we found in Malcolm's nightstand was very clear with what he wanted—me giving the final speech about his life and the musical trio in Unit G singing an upbeat song. Malcolm wanted to make sure everyone had a good time. Absolutely no tears. He stated in all caps that we were to celebrate his life, not mourn his death.

I clear my throat, thinking what to say about Malcolm, the self-declared gay mayor of Dallas. He is...*was*...flamboyant, bigger than life, and enjoyed every day to its fullest. Everyone loved him, especially me. His absence will leave an unimaginable void in us. Gray. Empty. Lonely.

What should I say about the man who saved me, gave me a

place to stay, and helped me find my purpose? I prepared something, but I can't seem to remember a single word. How to sum up the impact Malcolm had on me? I begin to ramble. "He meant the world…I would not be here…It's…It's so hard."

Martha grabs my hand. "We know how much you loved him, and he loved you. You were the son he always wanted."

"And he was my father in every way except for blood. Malcolm rescued me and many of you here."

"Amen," Martha says.

"You can do this, Oliver," Candy whispers. She's the only person present who doesn't live at Mockingbird Place. She's here for me.

Her encouragement helps me. I begin again. "I know how easily genetic ties can be loosened and tossed aside. So did Malcolm. We suffered similar fates, though decades apart, our families rejecting us and considering us outcasts. But our bond was stronger than blood. Our bond was a choice." I take a breath, unsure how to continue. And then it comes to me, as if Malcolm is reaching through the great beyond, the other side, the heavens or whatever it may be to help me get through his eulogy. I know he can't, but how much I long to hear his voice again. Still, it does feel like in some odd way he's close. I just need to use his words.

I look at my friends. "Malcolm Rivers was like no other man I've ever known. Generous. Kind. Understanding. He opened his home to me when I was at my lowest. I don't know what I would have…" I glance into the hole meant for his ashes and lose it. My own tears fall, as grief consumes me. "We are celebrating your life, Malcolm, but we miss you so much. Please understand why we can't help but cry."

Martha and Sarah put their arms around me as the thirteen of us stand quietly sharing our heartache.

I can't stop staring at the hole as my tears continue to stream down my face. Malcolm chose this very spot to be his final resting place, near the pool and only steps from Unit A, his home for the past fifty-nine years.

Malcolm's favorite kind of tree, a Bradford Pear that the nursery delivered earlier this morning, is ready to go into the ground on top of him. *So whenever you are in the pool and glance at the tree you might remember me.*

I have so many memories about him but wish I could have more.

I continue talking, though what I say is lost to me. My focus is muddled, like an out-of-body experience. I take the lid off the urn. As I begin pouring Malcolm's ashes into the earth, from the corner of my eye I see a stranger carrying a box and walking with a slight limp up the steps to Unit A.

Malcolm's home.

The guy trips and drops the box, which crashes to the ground. Its contents of glass are now shattered debris on the sidewalk.

We turn, and my grief morphs into uncontrollable anger. Though this rage is inappropriate, in the oddest way it distracts me from my pain, bringing back clarity, sharp and intense.

Once again in my body, I glare at the man who dropped the box and interrupted our memorial for my friend. "How dare he."

"What's wrong, Oliver?" Martha asks.

"Who is that clumsy asshole?" I point at the man.

She shrugs. "I don't know, but you shouldn't call him that. Accidents happen."

I know she is right, but holding onto the anger, misplaced or not, softens my sadness.

"Oh my God, M," Sarah says. "That's my fault. He's the new renter, Adam Stockton. When I gave him the keys and told him he could move in, I didn't realize it was the same day as Malcolm's last memorial. I'm so sorry."

"It's not your fault," I tell her, watching the guy walk out the door empty-handed, heading back to the parking lot. Was he just going to leave the mess on the sidewalk? That thought resuscitates my irritation, keeping my grief at bay. In my head I know it's not fair to our new neighbor to be so annoyed, but I can't help it. My emotions are raw and overwhelming.

Martha kisses Sarah on the cheek. "S, Oliver is right. It's not your fault. We've all been through so much."

Sarah wipes her eyes. "This is the hardest thing any of us has ever gone through. I miss Malcolm so much."

The new guy is ruining everything. I have to do something. I turn to Martha and Sarah, and the other ten. "Hold on a moment. Let me talk to him. Then we can place the tree together."

"I'll go talk to the asshole." Tony lives in Unit J and is a professional MMA fighter.

I know better than to send him. "Thanks, Tony, but I got this."

Tony's anger is like a beast that no cage can hold back when unleashed. I'll keep mine in check when I confront the new guy. At least I will try.

When I step up to Malcolm's front door, the new guy returns from the parking lot with a broom and dustpan.

"Hello," he says in a tone that is warm to my ears. "Sorry about the mess."

My anger subsides some, but I'm in no mood to be nice. "Do you mind holding off moving your shit in? We're conducting a memorial service for the man who lived in this unit."

He glances over at the others, who are consoling one another. "I didn't realize. Of course I can wait. I'm so sorry. I didn't know." He seems genuine. "A buddy who is supposed to help me with the bigger stuff will be showing up soon, but we'll wait until you are done. Is that all right?"

My anger is replaced by curiosity. Adam appears to be a very nice guy. "Yes. That will work."

There is something about him that draws me in. Is he genuine or is it only an act? And then I recall something Malcolm told me once. *A new friend, or boyfriend, often helps distract us from difficulties.*

Having to face the biggest *difficulty* of my entire life, I hold out my hand. "I'm Oliver Lancaster, Unit F." I point at my front door. "You know, the bottom of the U."

He shakes my hand firmly. "Adam Stockton, Unit A, but you know that already." He smiles. "The top right apartment of the U, next door to the laundry room."

I grin, liking his sense of humor. Unable to look away, I gaze into Adam's dark-brown eyes, the darkest I've ever seen. Almost black. His hair, also dark-brown, is short, much shorter than my own. What looks to me like three days without a razor, he has the most handsome, manly face I've ever seen. The jeans and T-shirt he wears cannot conceal the muscled frame underneath. He is ripped but not overly bulky.

I kneel down beside the rubble. "I hope nothing expensive was broken."

He kneels down next to me and sweeps up the big pieces of glass. "Just odds and ends. Nothing important."

I smile, still locking onto those eyes with the biggest lashes I've ever seen on a man. They are spread out like the handheld fans women of a previous generation used, and whenever he blinks I expect to feel a breeze. "Once we're done here, I'd be happy to help you finish moving in." I say it in part because I want to get to know more about him, and in another part because I want to get back inside Malcolm's apartment, a place I lived in until I turned twenty last year.

"I could use the help. Thanks, Oliver."

Hearing him say my name pleases me. I want to get to know him *a lot better*. "When we finish settling you in, I'll introduce you to the rest of your new neighbors. We're going to our favorite strip club on Cedar Springs tonight to toast the man we're saying goodbye to. Malcolm loved that club and the guys there are super hot."

Adam's expression changes from pleasant to hostile. "I'm not gay, Oliver."

I sense he is lying, but why? If he is, that makes me want to get to know him all the more. Closeted men have always been like warm flames on cold nights to me. "There's no law that says a straight man can't go into a gay club. See that guy and girl over there? That's Hayden and Lashaya Swan. They're your next-door neighbors. Unit B."

Hayden and Lashaya ended up at Mockingbird Place to escape another type of bigotry. Her parents did not approve of her marrying a white guy, and when she refused to break it off with Hayden, things turned really bad. But Malcolm pulled them in close to his special place of refuge, like he did me. *Mockingbird Place.*

"Hayden is straight and has no issues going to gay clubs."

"Good for him." Adam folds his arms over his chest, a clear sign he doesn't intend to go to the club. Ever.

But that only fuels my desire. Adam is a challenge, someone I can help seduce out of the closet, like I've done with others, Trent being my latest success story. "Come. You'll have fun. I promise."

"Don't you have a funeral to worry about?"

My grief slams back into the forefront of my mind, tightening my gut. For a brief moment I had forgotten what was happening by the pool. Again, I wonder how I'm going to survive without Malcolm. I'm still not sure, but I know Malcolm was right about one thing. A new friend might be just what I need to get through the next few days.

I smile at Adam. "We'll be done shortly. I'll be back to help you."

"Don't worry about it, Oliver. My buddy should show any moment."

Deciding not to push the issue, I say, "Great. I still would like to introduce you to the rest of the gang."

"Sure." His single syllable response is empty—hollow. Adam's stiffness remains.

Will I be able to chip away the walls he's built? He seems like a lost cause, but why? Regardless, I'm not willing to throw in the towel, at least not yet.

"See you around." Not waiting for him to respond, I return to the others.

"How did it go with the new guy?" Tony asks, his eyes dark and dangerous.

"Fine. Adam didn't realize we were having a memorial service. He's going to wait until we're done to move the rest of his things."

"He seems like a nice guy," Sarah says. "He recently got out of the Marines. I checked his references. He's actually a war hero."

That information definitely explains the buzz cut, and might also be the reason for his limp. There is so much more to Adam, so many layers, and I plan on exploring all of them.

"Shall we continue?" Candy asks, placing her arm around my shoulder.

"Yes," I answer. "Where was I?"

Hayden holds Lashaya close and says, "You were saying some nice things about Malcolm."

"That's right. Thanks, Hayden. Malcolm wants us to celebrate his life rather than mourn his death. No funeral. No casket. No crying. None. Even though we have shed many tears, let's try to send him off with smiles and laughter. I know it's difficult, but I'm desperately trying to keep my sadness in check. I hope you will too. It is the least we can do for him. That's what he deserves."

I say a few more words, glancing into Malcolm's final resting place, and then the trio starts singing their original song titled "It's All About Having Fun."

As they sing, the rest of us place the tree into the hole.

I look up into its branches and silently mouth, "Goodbye, my dear friend."

Chapter 2

Looking in the bathroom mirror, I check my hair and smile. I remember Malcolm teasing me about my vanity.

"You have thick, wavy blond hair many guys would die for, Oliver. Why does it take you thirty minutes to make sure not a hair is out of place? Just let it fall. I think men would find that extremely sexy."

"You're probably right," I say aloud to the empty room. I run my hands through my hair, creating a complete disaster. I laugh at my reflection. The messy hair reminds me of the styles I've recently seen on some good-looking guys at the clubs. "But you know me, Malcolm. I just can't let myself go."

I apply gel and tame my hair back into the style I prefer.

Taking one last look at my clothes, everything is in place, not a wrinkle in sight. I've been called uptight more than once. Perhaps it is true. But I have my reasons.

My cell buzzes.

It's Candy. God, I'm so glad to have her in my life. In fact, she's like a sister to me. She always has my back and I always have hers.

"Hey, you ready for me to come pick you up?" I ask.

"No, honey. I'm sorry, but I'm not going to be able to make the night out with you and your neighbors."

I'm very disappointed. Candy and I met in freshmen orientation and immediately hit it off. Having served in the Marines, she was older than most of the other freshmen students. Even though there is a five-year age difference between us, we couldn't be closer. We do everything together. Our run for the president and vice president positions on the Rainbow Student Coalition is just one example. We won by a landslide. I take my responsibility as president of the university's gay support group very seriously. Candy is just as dedicated as I am. And we both volunteer for the Lifeline Foundation, a local organization dedicated to helping gay and straight homeless teenagers get off the streets. Lifeline is very important to me.

"Why aren't you coming?" I ask.

"Melody and Ashley are very upset about something and wanted to talk to both of us. I told them about what you were dealing with so they agreed to talk with me alone."

"Do you know what they're upset about?" I think it might be something to do with the coalition, since Melody and Ashley are both members.

"They didn't say, but it sounded serious. Go have a drink with your neighbors. Raise a glass for me in honor of Malcolm."

"I will." I hate facing the rest of the night without Candy beside me. "You could come after you meet with Melody and Ashley."

"It'll be late. I need to get some rest. There's a ton left to do before the rally. Why don't you ask that good-looking Marine to go with you, Oliver?"

"You're just saying that because you Marines always stick together."

She laughs. "Very true."

"Actually, I was thinking about asking him for dinner tomorrow. What do you think?"

"That's a wonderful idea. Text me when you know."

"I will. One thing before you go, do you know who's checking the typical spots for Lifeline this weekend?"

"What did I tell you before, Oliver Lancaster?" She has that parental tone that always makes me laugh. "Me and the other volunteers are handling things for Lifeline. In fact, we found three homeless gay teens this week that we were able to get food and shelter for. Until things settle down for you, let us take care of the foundation. Besides, after your last close call saving that kid under that bridge in South Dallas, the executive director and the rest of the board are hesitant to let you get back out there."

"I took care of myself. Nothing happened. Those thugs took off."

"I know they did, but you aren't a superhero."

"I couldn't let them hurt him, could I?"

"No, but you shouldn't have been alone."

Saving homeless teens is my purpose. It gives meaning to my life. "Maybe not, but that's behind us now."

"Anyway, take care of yourself. You can get back to work with Lifeline next week. We have the coalition's rally to worry about right now. Have fun and get some rest. Love ya."

"Love ya more."

I click off the phone and it buzzes again.

I look at the screen and see Hayden's picture.

"I'm almost ready," I say as I answer. Deep down, I want to be alone. I really don't feel like going to the club—especially since Candy isn't going to be there with me—and think about telling him so. Because of the frenzy to get the activities Malcolm requested put together, I have held my emotions in check as much as possible. With everything over and done, I can let the anguish I've stuffed inside out. A bottle of wine and one of Malcolm's favorite movies is the perfect recipe to unlock my grief.

"Everyone is here but you, buddy. Hurry."

I'm not the only one suffering. The others aren't ready to face this alone, even if I think I am. Maybe I'm not ready either. Maybe I'm just trying to fool myself. Maybe I need them as much as they need me.

"I'm out the door." I click off the phone and put it in my pocket.

When I step out of my place, the rain begins to fall. I go back in and get my umbrella, grateful that we were dry during Malcolm's memorial by the pool.

I walk to my car and spot Adam alone trying to wrestle a chair out of a U-Haul truck with an empty tow dolly. A white Honda Pilot filled with clothes and sporting California plates is parked next to the truck. "Nice ride, Adam. You look like you could use some help. Where's your friend?"

"He didn't show." Adam shrugs. "Called in sick, so to speak." A smile appears on his handsome face. The earlier tension I sensed from him is gone. "I have to get this truck back by eight in the morning or pay for another day."

"So much for this umbrella." I fold it up and set it to the side.

"Aren't you meeting your friends?"

"I was." I remember how uptight he became when I mentioned the strip club. *I'm not gay, Oliver.* I bring out my cell. "I'll send them a text. They'll understand."

"Oliver, I can find someone else."

"Why bother since I'm here?" I send the text and put my phone away. "Let's get busy."

I roll up my sleeves and help him carry the chair to Unit A. We walk inside.

Adam and I put the chair down next to the front door.

It is so strange seeing the apartment without Malcolm's things. The only items inside are a few of Adam's boxes.

It seems like Malcolm is whispering to me that Unit A is no longer his, that it now belongs to Adam. I'm going to have to get used to calling this Adam's place. I'm not sure I will ever feel comfortable about that.

"Very different from when I lived here."

"You lived in this apartment? With the guy who died?"

"I did. Malcolm Rivers owned Mockingbird Place. He gave me my start here in Dallas." I can feel my grief creeping back in.

"Were you...I mean..."

"No. We weren't a couple, if that's what you were asking. He was like a father to me. And even though he was in his eighties, he was a blast to be around. The last party we had here was his eighty-second birthday. That was just a month ago, and only three weeks before he...before he..." I can't bring myself to say *before he died.* "Three weeks before Malcolm's heart attack."

Adam put his hand on my shoulder. "We don't have to talk about this now if it's too hard on you."

I look into his kind eyes and shake my head. "No. It's fine. Actually talking about him helps. We had so much fun celebrating his birthday. What a great party, though it wound down before ten. Unusual for Malcolm. A sign of what was to come with him that I should have noticed but didn't."

"I'm sorry you've gone through all this, Oliver. I really can do this by myself. It's got to be hard on you seeing me move into your friend's apartment, much less helping me do it."

His words melt my heart. Adam is one of the good guys.

"No. I want to help. Malcolm would want me to move on."

"Clearly a very wise man. Do you have a photo of him?"

I pull out my phone and bring up the pic of Malcolm and me standing next to his birthday cake.

"I like his smile and yours," Adam says.

"Malcolm told us he was tired and since we were all so young, we should go out to the clubs without him. He said it would be the best present any of us could give him. I stayed behind and helped him clean up. I had a strange feeling that something was wrong with him. But in typical Malcolm-fashion, after the last dish was put away, he insisted I go join everyone else. 'You're twenty-one, Oliver, not eighty-two. Go have fun.' God, I wonder if he knew what was coming."

"Whether he did or didn't, Malcolm obviously cared about you."

"Yes, he did. If I'd known I was going to lose Malcolm so soon, I would have refused to leave him. More than that even. I would have insisted on moving back into my old room here. It might have changed the outcome, even though the doctors told us there was nothing that could have saved him."

"Maybe this is hard to accept right now, and maybe I don't even have the right to say it—but what you've already told me about Malcolm, I believe he would not want you to beat yourself up with what-ifs. He would want you to be happy and think about the time you had together."

I look at Adam—really look at him. There is something very special about him. "You may not have known Malcolm but you're absolutely right. When I moved out almost a year ago I knew he was sad, though he never admitted it to me. In fact, Malcolm told *me* not to be sad. I put my arm around him and reminded him that we would only be a few doors away from each other. His eyes welled up. Then Malcolm told me we needed to remember what good times we had living together but not to dwell on the past."

"Why did you move into Unit F?" Adam asks.

"Malcolm thought I should have my own space. Told me I needed to spread my wings. I wasn't so sure. I liked living with him."

"He sounds like he was a terrific guy."

"He *was*." That word still makes me cringe when referring to Malcolm. Will I ever get used to it? I doubt it. "Even though I know he would have preferred for me to continue living with him, he never let on. That's the kind of man Malcolm Rivers was, always thinking of others and their needs."

"I wish I could have known him."

I smile. Why is it so easy for me to talk to Adam? "You would have liked him, and I know he would have liked you." I try to shake off the sadness so that we can get back to work. "Where do you want the chair?"

"I don't know. Where do you think it should go?"

"That corner by the window looks best right now, but a final decision can be made once the rest of your stuff is inside."

We are only able to get a few more of Adam's things into the apartment before the rain starts coming down hard.

"We better take a break until this slows down some." Adam reaches into a box marked *Bathroom* and pulls out a couple of towels.

I sit down on the wooden floor that once held Malcolm's large Persian rug.

Adam tosses a towel to me and begins drying off with another towel himself.

It's so nice to see him relax. Could I be wrong about him being gay? Maybe he isn't closeted. But something in my gut tells me otherwise.

"I've got wine but I haven't unpacked the glasses. I think they're still on the truck. There is beer in the fridge I bought for my buddy and me. Would you like one?"

I nod, noticing once again his slight limp as he walks to his refrigerator. "Sarah told me you're an ex-Marine."

"There are no *ex*-Marines, Oliver." He returns to the living room with two beers, sits down next to me on the floor, and hands me one. "There are two ways that inactive Marines are referred to. Me? I'm *former* Marine, since I didn't reach retirement. Far from it. I'm only twenty-two." He grins, making him appear even sexier than before, though I think that's impossible. "For those who did serve twenty-plus, we call them *retired* Marines."

"I've heard the saying 'Once a Marine, always a Marine.'"

"That's right. I bleed Marine green like my brothers and sisters." He holds up his beer. "Thanks for helping. I really appreciate it."

"My pleasure. Welcome to the neighborhood."

We clink our bottles together.

"Sarah told me you're a war hero."

"Hardly." Adam's earlier stiffness returns.

It's crystal clear to me that he doesn't want to talk about his military service, so I decide to drop the subject. "You're going to love Dallas. It's a great city."

"I'm sure I will. I've been here once on leave with friends. I had a lot of fun." His eyes lock with mine and I feel my temperature rise. "What brought you to Dallas, Oliver?"

Even though it's easy to talk to Adam, I'm not willing to share that part of my life with him. I don't share it with anyone. Malcolm is the only one who knows—*knew*—my whole story. So instead, I say, "I'm studying psychology at the university." It isn't a lie but it isn't answering his question directly. More of a white lie I suppose, but necessary. I've already unloaded too much about myself to him tonight.

"You're kidding." His eyes widen and then that gorgeous smile of his appears once again. "I'm enrolled for the second summer semester. My first time in college. That starts in one week."

"I'd be happy to show you around campus." I take a sip of my beer, keeping my eyes fixed on him. "It can be a little daunting at first."

Adam finishes his beer and places the empty bottle on the kitchen counter. My bottle is still over half full. I'm a little surprised at how fast he drank his.

He sighs, one of those long, heart-wrenching exhaling breaths that come from deep inside. "I bet I'm going to be the oldest freshman on campus."

"Not by a long shot. I had a sixty-two-year-old woman in my freshman English class." I remember how nervous I was before my first semester and hope I'm giving Adam something that will ease his concerns. "She told us that since her children and grandchildren had graduated, it was her turn to pursue her dreams. Great lady. And fun."

"That's really cool."

"And like you, there are lots of students that come to school after serving in the military. In fact my best friend was in the Marines like you. Candy was twenty-three when she enrolled."

"You're making me feel better." He walks into the kitchen and opens the refrigerator. "Ready for another?"

I down the rest of mine. Even though I'm not much of a drinker, if he's in the partying mood then I want to be in the partying mood. "Now I am."

"How long before you graduate?" he asks, handing me my second beer.

"I'm starting my senior year in the fall."

Malcolm's unique doorbell chimes *Le Nozze di Figaro*.

Adam looks surprised. "Is that Mozart?"

"Yes." I grin, realizing that Adam knows something about classical music. "It's *your* doorbell."

"Nice." Adam isn't anything like what I'd imagined a Marine would be—former or ex or whatever.

"That's from *The Marriage of Figaro*. Your doorbell also plays two other pieces by the composer. Malcolm loved Mozart."

"Looks like I really missed out on not getting to meet your friend. I'm really sorry you lost him."

His words of compassion wash over me like a healing balm. "You two would have gotten along very well."

Another Mozart piece begins to play.

"Doorbell? Someone's at my door." Adam laughs, which brightens my frame of mind even more. "I'm going to have to get used to this."

He walks to his front door, the limp barely noticeable now.

"Could that be your buddy?"

"Maybe, but I don't think so. He sounded really sick on the phone." He opens the door, revealing my friends, who had been waiting for me at the bar.

"Hi, Adam. I'm Martha Rivers and you've already met my partner Sarah. We got Oliver's text about your situation and brought reinforcements to help get you moved. And your neighbors are ready to pitch in."

Adam looks shocked at the outpouring of support. I remember my own reaction when I moved into Mockingbird Place. It was very similar.

Adam recovers quickly, the apparent shock dissipating, and opens the door wide. "Please. Come in."

Martha and Sarah lead the way, followed by Hayden and Lashaya, Trace and Jackson from Unit D, and entering last, is Tony.

Tony glares at Adam, which is quite intimidating given he has two black eyes. "Everyone but the doctor, fireman, and musicians are here." The guy has had a chip on his shoulder since he moved in eighteen months ago, though none of us know why.

But Tony's harshness doesn't seem to faze Adam.

Smiling, he holds out his hand. "I just appreciate any help. You look like you could use a beer, buddy."

"I sure could." Tony shakes his hand, but it is obvious he still doesn't trust Adam.

I'm fairly certain that Tony doesn't trust anyone.

Martha puts her arm around Tony. She is one of the few people he lets touch him. Looking at Tony, she says to Adam, "Dr. Jaris Black lives in Unit H. He's an intern at the hospital and works evenings and overnights. And Eli Grayson is a fireman. His hours are crazy. Eli lives in Unit C. And our sweet trio—Josh, Chad, and Franki—live in G."

"Just so you're not surprised when you meet the three of them, Franki is a girl," Sarah adds.

"But it's hard to tell," Tony states flatly. "Franki is a total dyke."

"Anthony Enzo Mantovani, stop it. Now." Martha frowns. "You're better than that. No more bigoted comments. Please."

"Whatever," he says. It is clear Tony doesn't like disappointing Martha, though it seems he doesn't give a damn about disappointing the rest of us.

Martha's smile returns. "Adam, Franki is a lesbian and she is a gorgeous young woman. The trio has a gig tonight or they would have been here to lend a hand. They are wonderful people."

"But very different from each other," Sarah says. "Josh is quiet and takes time to get to know, but once you do you'll have a friend for life. And Franki is extremely sweet and kind."

"And goes through girlfriends like potato chips," Tony interjects.

"She just hasn't found the right one," Martha says.

Sarah turns back to Adam. "The final ringleader of the band is Chad. He is over-the-top fun."

Tony says, "One thing for sure about those three—"

"Tony!" Martha warns in an I-mean-business tone.

"All I was going to say, Martha, is no matter how different they are, when the three of them play music together, it's amazing."

"I look forward to meeting them." Adam hands Tony a beer.

"I can't wait to see what this guy thinks of Chad." The smirk on Tony's face is met once again with disapproving looks from both Martha and Sarah.

I stand, placing my empty bottle next to Adam's. I look back at him and Tony. There seems to be an unspoken respect between the two of them. Why? I don't know but have a pretty good idea. Being an out and proud gay MMA fighter has to be tough. It's a sport dominated by chest-beating, testosterone-overflowing straight men. Seeing Tony with injuries isn't uncommon. I went to one of his matches with Malcolm. Tony's opponents suffer far worse in the fighting cage than he ever does. And Adam has certainly seen action on the battlefield, though he shows every sign of not wanting to talk about it. No wonder they are hitting it off from the very start.

There is so much more *I want* to know about Adam, but I'm not sure how to get *this former Marine* to open up and trust me.

"Hayden, take a picture of me and Oliver." Lashaya puts her arm around me.

Hayden takes several shots from his cell. "Got it, love."

"What was that for?" I ask.

She smiles. "I want to forever immortalize this night—the night Oliver Lancaster's hair wasn't perfect."

I laugh. "Blame the rain, Lashaya."

"I've been with you in the rain. Your hair has never looked like this before." She kisses me on the cheek. "Actually, I like this look on you. Casual suits you very nicely."

"You know me. Don't get used to it."

The rain ends and with everyone's help, we are able to unload the U-Haul, put together Adam's bed, and set up his bathroom.

Holding a box, Martha stands by the coat closet near the front door. "I don't remember a lock being on this before. Sarah, do you have key?"

"I don't have a key." Sarah looks puzzled and tries to turn the handle. It doesn't budge. "I don't remember this lock either."

"I put it on." Adam seems a bit guarded. "I placed my valuables in there earlier and completely filled it up. That box won't fit."

"Of course," Martha says. "Where would you like me to put it?"

"My bedroom closet." He smiles, appearing a little more at ease. "Thanks."

I wonder what kind of valuables Adam is storing behind that locked door. Why is he acting so secretive?

When Lashaya yawns, Adam asks, "What time is it?"

"Ten minutes to midnight," Hayden answers.

"I had no idea it was that late. Thank you so much for your help. I'll finish putting the rest away tomorrow. I'm certain by now we all could use some rest."

I stay behind as everyone says their goodbyes to him. I'm not ready to leave.

He hugs Martha and Sarah last. They wave to me, and then walk out.

When Adam shuts the door, I ask him, "How about another beer? There's three left."

"Actually, I'm hungry. Are you?"

"Starving."

He walks into the kitchen and holds up a grocery bag. "You like ramen noodles? I'm not much of a cook and I figured it might be too late to go out by the time I finished. I was right, even with all the help of our wonderful neighbors and you."

This will be our first meal together. "Noodles and beer? Sounds perfect."

Adam laughs. "I even got cupcakes for dessert. Now all we need to do is find a pot in one of these boxes so we can boil the noodles."

A few minutes later, our dinner is ready to eat.

He looks in several boxes. "I found forks but no plates or bowls. Oh, well. I guess we'll have to eat out of the pot. And since my dining room table is loaded with boxes and my new sofa won't be delivered until tomorrow, we'll have to sit on the floor." He walks into the living room, carrying a couple of forks and our pot of noodles.

I plop down in the same place I sat in before everyone else arrived. "It'll be like an indoor picnic."

He laughs, sits down next to me and then scoots even closer. So close my heart skips a beat.

Adam holds the pot out for me. "You take the first bite."

Heat rushes through me as I twirl my fork in the pot. I wonder if he realizes how intimate this feels. Was my first instinct about him right? Is he gay? I'm confused. I'm not about to bring up that subject now, especially remembering how he acted when I mentioned the gay strip club. Right now I must be patient with him. I like Adam. If he isn't gay, I hope we can at least be friends. But if he is...well, that is a different story.

As I taste the noodles, his eyes are fixed on me. "How did I do, Oliver?"

"Delicious." I haven't eaten ramen noodles in a very long time. Malcolm was an excellent cook and taught me everything he knew about the kitchen. We always ate like kings. "It has a flavor I can't quite figure out."

Laughing, Adam places his arm around me. "It's beer. I'm no chef and I don't have any spices except salt and pepper, but I thought if I poured some of my beer in the pot it might make our noodles taste better."

"It does taste great. Good idea."

"Really? You're not just saying that, are you?"

"Yes. Really." I smile at his enthusiasm. I've witnessed a sliver of his dark side when he adamantly stated he wasn't gay. But now, he seems completely relaxed and open. This seems to be another side to his personality. How many sides does he have? Adam is still a mystery to me.

We polish off the entire pot of noodles quickly.

"I guess we were hungry." He finishes his beer and remains next to me. "Ready for dessert?"

I would much rather taste his lips, but for now, I will settle for a cupcake. "I would love dessert."

He jumps to his feet, collecting our two forks and the empty pot, and returns to the kitchen.

Again, I notice his slight limp. I really wish I knew what happened to him. But if I say something it might end the evening, and I don't want it to end. We've only had a little time alone together. I want more, but feel if I stay much longer, I will screw things up.

He brings the cupcakes on a napkin. "There's a chocolate and a vanilla. Which one do you want?"

I look into his dark eyes, wondering what it would be like to hold him close. "Chocolate, please."

"That's my favorite, too." He sits down even closer to me than before, the sides of our legs touching with only the fabric of our jeans keeping our skin apart.

My heart begins to race. "How about we cut the cupcakes in two, Adam, and split them? That way we both get a taste of our favorite."

He laughs in such a way I can't help but smile. It's hearty and warm. "Oliver, you're a genius."

He takes a bite of his chocolate slice and closes his eyes. "Mmm."

I can't help but stare at the drop of icing that is on his thick lips. When his tongue appears and sweeps it into his mouth, I think I'm going to pass out. He is the hottest guy I've ever met. I need to get control of myself or my excitement will get the better of me.

Adam's eyes pop open. "What are you waiting for? It's delicious."

I take a bite of mine. In the sexiest voice I can muster, I say, "It is so delicious—sweet, moist, and creamy."

"You should be the bakery's spokesperson. Have you ever thought about doing commercials?"

So much for trying to sound sexy, but I'm not ready to give up. Not yet. "No, I never have."

"You should consider it. You've got a great voice."

"Thanks. This has been a blast, Adam."

"A blast?" He grins again. "I'm glad but I feel like I've taken advantage of you. This has been a lot of work."

Please take advantage of me. "Next time I want to cook dinner for you."

"That would be great. I'll bring a six-pack or a bottle of wine. But don't think you have to top my meal." He grins, holding up his remaining cupcake half. "This is five-star dining at its best."

"Yes, it is. And the company can't be beat." Despite how much I want to stay, I wrap up the remainder of my dessert in the napkin. "It's late. I better go."

A flash of disappointment appears on his face and then quickly vanishes. He gets up on his feet. "Thanks, buddy. Without your help and all the other neighbors pitching in, I wouldn't have been able to get the truck unloaded." He holds out his hand in the universal gesture of friendship.

Is this all we are ever going to be? Just friends?

I can't resist testing the water, just a little. "Come on, buddy. We've shared noodles. We're friends who deserve a hug." I pull him in and he doesn't resist.

It still doesn't confirm my suspicions about him, but it does give me a reason to hope.

He steps back and smiles. "It is late and I have to get up early to take the truck back."

I nod, realizing the night with him is coming to an end. I can't remember ever having more fun with anyone before.

He walks me to his door, his limp reminding me he is a hero. I want to know more about that. Maybe tomorrow night he will be comfortable enough to tell me.

He opens the door and we step out of Unit A—*A for Adam's place, not Malcolm's*. "Thanks again, Oliver."

"How about dinner tomorrow night? My place. Do you like steak?"

"I love steak."

"Medium-rare?"

He smiles. "Medium to medium-well. What time?"

"Seven."

"See you then." He steps back inside, his eyes locking on mine for a brief moment. A moment that I wish could last forever. "Goodnight."

The door closes.

I look at my watch. It is one-thirty in the morning, later than I usually take my evening swim. But I need to cool off, need to think. The rain clouds are gone. The water will be cold, but that's never stopped me before. I walk to my apartment and change into my trunks.

Chapter 3

All twelve units at Mockingbird Place are two-story with front and back doors. They have small private patios just outside their kitchens. Unlike the open public spaces of the courtyard and pool, where we congregate together for parties or just to hang out, our patios have eight-foot high privacy fences. Believing everyone deserves an outside quiet space of their own, Malcolm put them in many years ago.

I love mine.

Malcolm bought me the gas grill as an apartment-warming gift. Martha and Sarah's present was the patio furniture. The rest of my neighbors gave me potted plants and flowers.

I fire up the grill and wipe the grate down with oil so the rib eye steaks will get those gorgeous dark marks. I want to impress Adam.

I'm excited about having him over. Even after my swim last night I had trouble falling asleep. My mind wouldn't shut down but kept replaying every second I spent with him. I wanted to catch him before he had to return the rental truck but didn't awake until after eight. By then he was already gone. So much for me offering him donuts and coffee.

Malcolm's former advice reminds me I shouldn't be so obsessive.

Oliver, you get too intense when you first meet a guy. Take your time. Enjoy the journey.

My cell rings. I look at the caller ID. The call is from Candy.

I think about letting her call go to voicemail because I know she would understand since I sent her a text about my dinner plans with Adam.

Even though he will be arriving soon, I decide to answer. "Hey."

"I know I need to make this quick since your Marine neighbor is about to come over to your place, but this is important."

"What's up?"

"Oliver, we may have an issue with the vote on the new mission statement for the charter. My meeting with Melody and Ashley didn't solve their issues. They want to talk with you and me tomorrow to continue discussing their concerns."

"I thought we'd already answered all their questions."

"So did I, but clearly they still aren't convinced we should make the change."

"I never dreamed that going from LGBT to LGBTQIA would be so difficult."

I'm proud of Candy and my effort to include QIA in our charter. Adding those three letters brings in new groups to our organization: questioning, gender queer, intersex, asexual and ally.

"Neither did I, but they are still hung up on the term 'queer.' "

Melody and Ashley are from small towns like me. I understand their hesitation. It's all about the letter Q and part of what it will stand for. The questioning group isn't the problem, but gender *queer* is. Not the group, but that one word. Traditionally, the word queer is derogatory and hurtful. I was called "queer" and "fag" and so many other slurs when I still lived at home. But Malcolm gave me a new perspective on the term. *We have the power to claim that word as our own. So many young people who do not adhere to sexual or gender norms are using it to self-identify in a positive way. Those terrible things that happened to you in your past made you the man you are today. You are stronger than a single word, Oliver.*

"Candy, I think it's important we hear Melody and Ashley out before we vote in the fall."

"I agree. When can we meet with them?"

"Tomorrow, after our rally in front of Dallas Hall."

"Perfect. Thanks, Oliver."

"Love ya."

"Love ya more."

After the call ends, I place the thick rib eye steaks on the grill. The sizzle and aroma that follow whet my appetite. *Ten minutes before Adam arrives.*

My patio table is set with fresh flowers as a centerpiece. The temperature is seventy-two, cool for this time of year. The forecast calls for clear skies. The chocolate cake is iced. The bottle of wine is sitting on the table. It's Malcolm's favorite that he always served with steak.

Everything is ready and perfect for my dinner with Adam.

My doorbell chimes. *He's a little early.*

I close the grill's lid and rush to welcome Adam to my home.

When I open the door, it isn't Adam standing in front of me, but one of my neighbors from Unit D—Trace Cotton. Trace and his roommate Jackson also helped unload Adam's truck last night.

"Sorry to bother you, Oliver, but I accidently locked myself out of my place."

Trace has long black hair with a dark complexion and light blue eyes. He is quite handsome. He has a laid-back personality about most things that I admire, except when it comes to his paintings. He is an art major. But for some strange reason that I still don't understand, he never shows his work to anyone. I've only seen one of his paintings, and that one strictly by accident. It was so beautiful. He's incredibly talented. It was of a beach scene with families enjoying the warmth of the sun and coolness of the ocean. It was the middle of winter when I saw it, and I felt like I could walk right onto the sand Trace had created with his paints and brushes. When I asked him why he'd never shown anyone his work, Trace answered that it was difficult to explain. I've never seen that painting or any others of his again.

"Jackson is at the store getting things for our party tomorrow night," Trace says.

He and Jackson initially hooked up when they first met. They realized early on that they weren't meant for each other but still ended up being best friends and roommates.

Trace asks, "Do you mind if I borrow our key back from you?"

"Of course. Come on in." I take him to the drawer I keep my neighbors' keys in.

I have all of them except for three units.

Tony doesn't exchange keys with anyone except Martha and Sarah.

I also don't have a key to Unit E, which is still vacant. It's between Trace and Jackson's apartment and mine.

And I no longer have a key to Unit A, *Adam's place*. Where is Adam? Shouldn't he be here by now?

I lift Unit D's key out of the drawer. It is on a key ring in the shape of an Egyptian ankh with the bottom broken off, definitely purchased by Trace, not Jackson. Jackson is like me. Serious. Detailed. More than a little OCD. Jackson would have thrown out the broken key ring and replaced it.

"What smells so good?" Trace asks.

"I've got steaks on the grill. I've invited Adam over."

"Ah. Interesting. He's good-looking and seems really nice. Is he gay?"

"Not sure. He claims he isn't."

"Uh-huh." Trace smiles. "That's just your type. Closeted. Seems like you have a few things to work out."

More than you know. "Let's go out on my patio. I need to turn the steaks."

"I better get out of here before your guest arrives. We don't want him thinking you and I are a couple."

We laugh.

"I'll let myself out, Oliver. Thanks for the key. I'll get it back to you tomorrow."

After I flip the rib eyes, my cell buzzes with a text from Adam.

Sorry for the late notice, Oliver, but I won't be able to make dinner tonight.

I'm confused and worried, so I type back, *What's wrong?*

No response, which concerns me. Has something happened to

him? He is new to Dallas. There are places in the city that can be dangerous, especially if you don't know where you are.

Adam, please answer me. Do you need my help?

I take the perfectly cooked steaks off the grill and back into the house. Still no answer.

Anxiously, I fire off another text to him. *Adam, are you there?*

A moment later my cell buzzes with his answer. *I'm fine. I just don't want to have dinner with you.*

I reread the text several times, which only confuses me more. *I don't want to have dinner with you.* With me? What the hell?

I'm pissed and hurt. What happened between now and after I left him last night? What has changed Adam's mind about having dinner with me? I look at the steaks, which are a luxury. I may own part of Mockingbird Place now, but that doesn't make me rich. I'm a college student that still has to depend on loans, grants, and what I earn at my part-time job at the university just to get by. I don't have family to lean on. Malcolm has been my only family. Hell, I wouldn't have been able to afford my place if Malcolm hadn't cut the rent by half.

How can Adam be so thoughtless? If he's had a change of heart, he should have called me earlier.

I'm not about to let the meal I prepared go to waste. I pull out some plastic containers to pack up our food—one container for Adam's portion and one for mine. I'm in no mood to eat now. I'm seething on the inside as I cut a big slice of chocolate cake. My plan is to march his food to Unit A and make him see the trouble I've gone to for our dinner. Let him see what he has turned away.

What the hell is the matter with me? I have every right to be irritated. I cooked a big meal for us. But I'm so much more than irritated. I'm totally pissed. Why? It doesn't make any sense to me. I just met the guy. Maybe I'm better off that this happened now and not down the road. I'm done with his mixed signals. Gay or straight, Adam is being a complete ass.

My doorbell rings.

"Who the hell can that be now?" I love my neighbors but don't feel like being around any of them at the moment.

When I open the door, I'm shocked to see Adam standing there. My first feeling is to slam the door in his face. But instead I act like a gentleman, waiting to hear what he has come to say.

"Oliver, I'm sorry. I'm a jerk."

"We can agree on that." I'm not about to hide my anger from him.

"There is no excuse for my bad behavior. Could we still have dinner?"

"What changed your mind since you sent me that text just five minutes ago?" My fury swirls inside me like a fallen beehive, but I've learned that it only hurts me when I can't let it go. Another of Malcolm's teachings.

"I read my text to you and realized how abrupt I was being." Adam's tone seems full of sincere regret.

I look into his dark eyes, and a little bit more of my anger subsides. "Come inside. I'll listen to what you have to say." I still am not ready to decide whether to have dinner with him or not.

Adam walks into my apartment. "I like your place." He looks around my unit, which is decorated with a modern esthetic.

"I like sleek lines and minimalism. It suits me. But are you here to discuss my sense of style or did you want to talk about something else?"

"Straight to the point. I like that about you, Oliver. Where do I begin? Like I said before, there is no excuse, but I had a really screwed up day. First, I got turned around trying to get the truck back to the rental lot off of Harry Hines. I ended up arriving fifteen minutes late and the prick behind the desk wouldn't wave the charge for an extra day. Then the cable company was supposed to show up after nine. They showed up at 8:30. I was at the rental company at the time. So I have to reschedule an appointment for next week. When I got home, I started unloading my boxes and ended up dropping the one that held my grandfather's antique clock. It's broken and I'm not sure it can be fixed. Then right before I headed over here, my mother called and informed me she was going to drive to Dallas to see my place. She'll be here early next week, and I haven't a clue how to set up my apartment. I was so upset with everything that happened today I took it out on you. I'm so sorry." His eyes lock on mine. "Will you still feed me, Oliver?"

Hearing this big Marine hero suddenly sound like a small boy who'd been caught with his hand in the cookie jar makes me smile. "Yes, I'll feed you. And I'll do better than that. I will help you put your apartment together. You already said that you like my place. You do, don't you?"

Without warning, Adam hugs me. "I love your place."

I hug him back, inhaling his masculine scent and relishing the feel of his strong arms around me.

He pats me on the back and releases me. "So, buddy, am I forgiven?"

"Yes, but don't ever do that again." *Buddy?* I'm confused again. Is he gay or isn't he?

"I won't. I really could use your help decorating. God, what smells so good?"

"Our dinner. Lucky for you I didn't throw it in the trash."

"Very lucky for me."

I lead him to the patio. "I thought it would be nice to dine alfresco."

"Wow. This looks nice. I love eating outdoors. It makes the food taste better, at least it always did for my military rations."

I'm glad he's talking about his service. I'm hopeful I will get to learn a lot more about the mysterious Marine in Unit A. "Would you mind opening the wine while I bring out our food?"

He grabs the bottle and opener off the table. "I don't mind at all, my friend."

Friend. Buddy. Damn.

When I return, I find him sitting at the table with a wine glass to his gorgeous lips. He stands and hands me a glass. "For the chef."

"Thanks." I take a sip, enjoying the sweetness of the Malbec. "Do you like it?"

"Very much. I normally don't drink wine, but this is very good." He grins. "Who knows? The more we hang out, the better chance I get at becoming a wine connoisseur. Does that sound good, buddy?"

"Sure, *buddy*." I like that he wants to spend more time with me but I hate that he keeps calling me *buddy*. "I'm going to put our steaks back on the grill for sixty seconds to warm them up. They may come out a little more done but the heat will bring out the flavor. I'll add a little butter to keep them from being too dry. Then they'll be fine."

"Much better than the Ramen noodles I served you last night. As you know, my secret ingredient for everything is beer." Again, a mischievous look appears on his face. "Have you thought about pouring a little on the steaks?"

"Not this time, but I have used beer in several recipes. It's too late to use beer now, but maybe next time."

He busts out laughing. "I was kidding, Oliver. I just learned how to operate an electric can opener a few months ago. A kitchen is a more foreign place to me than the deserts of the Middle East."

"Is that where you served?" The moment the words pass my lips I wish I could pull them back.

Adam closes his eyes. "Yes. Afghanistan."

I'm certain that he's picturing the place in his mind. What horrors did he see and suffer over there? "If you don't want to talk about—"

"It's okay." He opens his eyes and takes another sip from his glass. "This tastes great. What kind of wine is this?" He picks up the bottle and looks at the label.

The abrupt change of topic makes it apparent that despite Adam saying it's okay, he still isn't ready to talk about his time in the Marines.

"I'm glad you're enjoying it. It's an Argentinean Malbec. It's one of my favorite reds."

During our meal, he leads the conversation, asking me about the university and about Mockingbird Place. It's strange that he never asks me about my family, where I was born, my tastes in music, places I've been, or anything else about me. Those are the normal getting-to-know-you questions I'm familiar with from new friends. Does he want to know more about me? I definitely want to know more about him. Worried I might scare him off, I don't ask him anything personal, past or present. It's painfully clear certain topics are not up for discussion. Is this because he's hiding something? Is he gay? Will he ever tell me?

It isn't like me to bite my tongue in this kind of situation. Normally I come right out and ask a guy like him if he is gay. If that offends anyone, I don't care. That's their problem not mine. Except when it comes to Adam—I do care. Why?

My ex, Trent, was shocked when I asked him if he was gay. He even cussed me out. Two weeks later, Trent was marching next to me in the gay pride parade.

I'm proud of who I am.

I came out at a young age in a conservative family and paid a very high price for it. My truth means something to me. Maybe that is why I seek out guys in the closet. I want them to feel the freedom I feel.

I sense Adam is gay, and I mean to find out *his truth* no matter how long it takes me. I'm attracted to him. What guy wouldn't be? I can be patient.

"God, this was so good, Oliver." Adam gathers our empty plates. "And your chocolate cake is the best I've ever had. Delicious."

"I'm so glad you liked it."

Together, we put everything away. After I start the dishwasher, I turn to him. "So, shall we get started on setting up your place?"

His eyebrows shoot up. "Are you kidding me? Now?"

"You said yourself that your mother is going to be here next week."

He groans. "Don't remind me."

"Is she that terrible?"

"She's not terrible. Quite the opposite. Mom is amazing."

That Adam has a mother he loves is one of the few things I now know about him. I also know he's a former Marine and is about to start college. Other than that, I'm still in the dark.

Hoping to nudge him to give me more, I say, "Tell me about your mother."

"Mom had to raise me as a single parent when my dad was killed in combat. I was still an infant."

"That's terrible." Though what I'm hearing saddens my heart, I feel so lucky to get a glimpse of who he is and why.

"My mom went back to college and got her degree. She was a teacher. Every summer she took graduate courses until she received her Master's and became a principal. She's so driven." Adam smiles, the pride for his mother shining through. "Mom continued her education and now has her PhD. She's the superintendent for the school district back home. So now do you understand why I need everything to be perfect for her?"

"Of course I do. She's does sound amazing." I'm stunned that he is sharing such personal details about his past. "You've come to the right person to help decorate your place. Ask anyone around here. I know how to make things perfect. I'm a little OCD."

Adam smiles and puts his arm around my shoulder. "If OCD gets my apartment looking a tenth as nice as yours, bring it on."

"Let's get to work."

We go to his apartment.

"Oliver, my stuff may not give you much to work with."

"I saw most of your things, and they are quite nice." Excitement rolls through me that I will get to spend more time with him. "I can work magic. Trust me."

He unlocks the door and we walk inside.

"Let me get us a couple of beers before we get started." Adam goes into the kitchen.

Ready to begin decorating, I scan his place. The first thing I notice is the coat closet is unlocked and opened. It isn't packed like he claimed last night. In fact it only holds three items, which explains Adam's limp.

Three prosthetic legs.

One has a natural skin tone. The other two are unusual, one metal and one black. They seem to be for the same leg, the left one. From the sizes, it appear that they fit just below the hip. *Below Adam's hip.*

"I think we should start in the guest bedroom where my—" Holding two beers, Adam stops in the middle of the living room.

I look away from the closet, but obviously I'm not quick enough since his face holds an oh-my-God-I've-been-found-out expression.

Hoping to alleviate his apparent concern that I've found out his secret, I say, "The guest room is a great place for us to start."

Adam frowns and sits down the bottles on the coffee table. "Oliver, I know you saw them."

My gut tightens. How do I get out of this mess? What can I say that will get him to trust me? "Yeah, I saw your legs. The door was open. So what? Doesn't matter to me."

"Well, it matters to me." He picks up one of the bottles and shoves it in my chest. "Take your beer and go." Adam is in full-on military mode, barking orders at me. "And don't ever tell anyone what you saw or I will know where it came from."

"What the fuck, Adam? It's no big deal, but I won't tell anyone if you don't want me to."

"It *is* a big deal. I'm not the man I was." He glares at me, his face storming with dark emotion.

Is this his secret? That he's lost a leg? Maybe he isn't gay. Maybe he is just a guy who has sacrificed so much that he feels broken.

"You're right, Adam. In one sense it is a big deal. You lost your leg, I assume in battle."

"I did, but what does that matter. In battle. A car wreck. Falling off a fucking cliff. Whatever. It's the same. My leg is gone. I should have been killed, like my dad. That would have made everything so much easier."

The pain in his voice crushes me. He's suffered so much. I want to hold him, comfort him, to tell him something that will make him feel better. But what can I say? I'm not sure but I know I must try. "What you did for me, for all of us, for the entire country is extraordinary. It's an honor to know you. You are a hero."

"I'm not a fucking hero." He slams the closet door shut. "Just leave."

"Please, Adam. Just talk to—"

"I. Said. Go. "

He's giving me no choice, so I turn and walk out the door of Unit A.

Chapter 4

A little before one in the morning I finish my last lap in the pool, but it hasn't helped me settle down. I remain a complete wreck.

I had thought about texting Candy right after leaving Adam's place but didn't. Her plate is too full already dealing with getting the rally ready.

Treading water in the deep end, I glance at Adam's windows once again. All the lights are still off. Obviously, he isn't so upset that it's keeping him awake—*like it is me.*

What could I have done differently? *Not look in the damn closet, Oliver.*

I like Adam. I like him a lot. And even if he is gay, there doesn't seem like there's any chance for a relationship after what happened. Of course I'm only good for a month, maybe two, as a boyfriend. Any longer just isn't in the cards for me. Breakups are tough but are my necessary evil. Trent and I have remained friends, but I'm not sure that would happen with Adam if things miraculously turned out differently for us. God, I would love to be his boyfriend, even if only temporarily. So what does it matter? Maybe it's better this way. But inside I wish I could be more for Adam, that we could have something permanent. Not possible. Not for me, no matter how much I'm attracted to him, no matter how much I wish things could be different.

Whether Adam is gay or straight, I want to be friends with him. But is that even possible now? He is so pissed that I've seen his prosthetic legs. I replay what happened over and over in my mind, but of course that isn't going to change anything.

I look at the pear tree we planted for Malcolm. I need his advice now more than ever before.

Martha steps out of hers and Sarah's apartment, Unit I. She waves at me and lights a cigarette. She and Sarah never smoke in their home or in any of ours.

I get out of the pool and dry off. The wind picks up, chilling my skin and shaking the leaves of the little tree.

Martha is Malcolm's cousin. Maybe she can help me figure a way out of this mess.

I walk up to her. "Can't sleep?"

"Mr. Arthur Ritis decided to show up and make my joints ache. I know you haven't met him yet, Oliver." She smiles. "I hope you never do because he always shows up, especially when you don't want him too. I was tossing and turning and thought I might wake Sarah, so I decided to get up and put on a pot of coffee and take one of my pills. I hate taking the damn things, but every once in a while I just have to."

"I'm actually glad you're up, Martha. I need your advice. I accidently found out a secret about Adam, and he was so mad at me he made me leave."

"I bet you're talking about his artificial leg."

I'm shocked she knows. Has Adam confided in her and Sarah? "How did you find out?"

She takes a drag on her cigarette. "I've been around a long time. Few things get past these old eyes, but truthfully, it's because of my father that I figured out Adam's secret. My father lost his leg in World War II and had the same gait as Adam, especially going up and down stairs. Not all amputees walk the same, but Adam's injury must be very similar to my father's, which left him very little leg below the hip. Apparently Adam hasn't quite accepted losing his leg yet." She sighs. "My father never accepted it. Of course, the military didn't have counseling back in those days like they do now. My father became a mean and hateful man and treated me terribly."

Seeing the ancient pain in her eyes like I'd seen in Malcolm's, I grab her hand and squeeze. Malcolm's parents disowned him after learning he was gay. Martha's did the same to her when she'd confided in them about her truth.

"You're such a sweet young man." Martha takes another puff from her cigarette and then puts it out. "I'm certain Adam's had counseling, but sometimes these things take a long time. He just needs lots of love."

"He told me his mother is coming. Maybe her being here with him will help. That's how this all started. He wants to impress his mom and asked for my help decorating his apartment. We were having such a good time and then everything went to hell." I tell her about seeing the prosthetics in the closet. "I wouldn't have hurt him for the world. I'm a psychology major and can't figure this out. So what do I do now?"

"You know you cannot fix this for Adam. He's got to figure it out on his own. All you can do right now is to be a good neighbor and friend. He'll come around. He just needs a little space. Be patient. You'll see. Does that make sense to you?"

"Martha, you know me. I'm going to do what you said and give him space, but I don't have any patience. I want to go over there right now and make him see how valuable a person he is."

"But you won't, will you?"

I sigh. "No. I won't."

"Speak of the good-looking devil. Don't turn around, but Adam just stepped out of his apartment and is sitting down on the steps." She waves at him.

"I guess he couldn't sleep after all." Despite her telling me to stay put, I turn around and see Adam waving back at Martha. "Why did you have to wave at him?"

"Because I didn't want him thinking you had told me his secret."

"I didn't tell you," I whisper, unable to turn away from Adam.

He looks like he is hurting. I hate it and wish I could take away his pain.

"Quit staring at him, Oliver. Give him his space. If you don't, you will end up never having a chance with him."

I turn back to her. "What do you mean by that?"

"I've never seen you act this way about anyone before. You're attracted to him. Don't even try to deny it."

"I wouldn't dare try, but I don't know if he's gay. In fact, he told me he wasn't."

She grins. "Come inside. Have coffee with me. We're both wide-awake. I could use the company and so could you."

We walk into her apartment. The only lights on are in the kitchen. We sit at the table and she pours each of us a cup of coffee.

"Do you think Adam's gay?" I ask her.

"I don't think he's gay, Oliver. I *know* he's gay."

"How?"

"The same way I knew about his leg. Living as long as I have gives a person insight to things you can't imagine. For instance, you and Adam would be perfect together, and I'm not just talking about a hookup, Oliver. I'm talking about building a life side by side."

She doesn't know why that isn't possible for me.

"Martha, you are a hopeless romantic."

"These are exciting times. Everyone expects the Supreme Court to rule in our favor. Wouldn't it be great if you two could get married right here in Texas?"

"OMG, Martha. Isn't that getting the horse and the cart mixed up? That's how you say it, right?"

She laughs. "The saying is 'getting the cart before the horse.' It means jumping the gun."

"Jumping the gun?"

"Oh, you know what I mean. I forget how young you are. Um. Let me see. This isn't working. The long and short of it…I'm doing it again."

I laugh. "I'm the one who brought it up. I may not have said it right but I do know what it means. Adam and I haven't even kissed and you're dreaming of our wedding?"

"Maybe so, but I know what I know. And if you two don't *F* it up, pardon my French, you might end up getting the happily ever after like Sarah and I have."

"I heard ya'll talking." Wearing purple pajamas, Sarah walks from the dark living room to the kitchen. "Do either of you realize what time it is?" She yawns.

Martha stands and hugs her. "Sorry, sweetheart. We didn't mean to disturb you. It's just that Oliver asked for my advice when I stepped out to smoke a cigarette."

"Oh, is there a problem with Adam?"

"Are both of you psychic?" I ask.

"Just wise, Oliver. Very wise." Sarah sits down. "M, would you pour me a cup. Smells delicious."

"S, you know what caffeine does to you."

"There's no chance of me going back to sleep now."

"Me either." Martha kisses her, gives her a cup, and sits down.

Martha and I fill Sarah in on everything that has happened between Adam and me.

Sarah sighs. "Poor Adam. He's just got to figure this out on his own. Oliver, I know you want to fix this for him but you can't. The best thing for you to do is to give him a little time. He will come around."

"Did you two rehearse this? Martha told me almost the exact same thing."

She smiles and grabs Martha's hand. "No rehearsing necessary. We've been together for so long we can finish each other's sentences." Then she leans forward. "And remember, we are wise. I did tell you that, didn't I? We are wise as owls."

Martha starts laughing.

"Honey, what's so funny?" Sarah asks.

I wonder too.

Martha turns to me, still laughing. "Sarah and I have lots of experience. Experience is the mother of wisdom. We weren't born yesterday. We know how to hit the nail on the head."

I start laughing at her string of idioms.

"I don't get what's so funny," Sarah says, which only sends Martha and I into a deeper state of hysterics.

It feels good to laugh. It's the release I needed, though I'm still worried about Adam.

"Idioms, S. That is what Oliver and I are laughing about."

"I still don't get it."

Martha and I laugh until tears stream down our faces, and Sarah, despite not really understanding what is so funny, starts laughing with us.

When I gain my composure, I say, "Martha, I guess it's true that laughter is the best medicine."

"Oh, I get it." Sarah grabs Martha's hand. "Arthur came to visit you and you needed to laugh."

Martha giggles. "I really didn't think about it but I do feel better. How about you, Oliver?"

"A little, thanks to you both."

After we say our goodbyes and I walk beside the pool to my place, I'm still grinning. But a single glance at Unit A's dark windows and the empty steps that Adam had been sitting on reminds me how he and I left things. Not good.

I step inside my apartment. Like Sarah said, there will be no sleeping tonight. I turn on my laptop and start going over my speech for the rally tomorrow. But my mind is on one thing and won't let it go, no matter how hard I try to force it to focus on the task at hand.

Are Martha and Sarah right about Adam and me? That we belong together? They say they know he's gay. Are they right about that too? Do I need to just give him time and he will come around? I'm not sure but don't know what else I can do.

Chapter 5

After being awake all night, I step out of the shower. The rally doesn't start until noon, but I need something, *anything* that can distract me from thinking about what happened with Adam. Giving him space is what Martha and Sarah think I should do, so I decide to let a single day pass. But if I don't hear from him by tomorrow, I will make the first move to fix things between us. And besides, Adam still needs help setting up his apartment before his mother arrives, and I want to be that help.

I finish getting ready and take one last look at my hair before leaving my apartment.

I park my car in the student parking lot.

The university I attend has a large green space in the middle of campus. Mature trees line the sidewalks that are sparsely filled with students going to and from their classes and dormitories. In the fall the grounds will be teeming with students.

I look at the time on my cell. 8:21am. I have over three and a half hours to kill before the rally. Where to go? The library? No. I didn't need to go over my speech any more, since I've spent several early morning hours already working on it. I'm ready. So I decide to get a bite of breakfast in the cafeteria.

When I walk inside, I see Adam at a table filling out some paperwork. I freeze in place. I'm in a quandary whether to approach him or not, whether to follow Martha and Sarah's advice or not, whether to tamp down my desire to sit down next to him to say how sorry I am—*or not.*

Adam looks at me. Did he feel me staring at him? Before I can step back to the entrance to leave, he waves me over. I feel my shoulders relax as relief rolls through me. At least he is willing to talk to me again. I take cautious steps in his direction. Gone are his jeans and T-shirt and facial hair. He is clean-shaven, wearing black slacks and a white dress shirt and blue tie. Casual or dressed up, with whiskers or without, Adam is the epitome of masculine beauty.

"Have a seat, Oliver."

I do, waiting for him to lay into me again about seeing his prosthetic legs.

But instead he asks, "Would you mind if I put your name down as a reference on this application? They're asking for a student or professor's name. You're the only one I know." He looks at me with those damn gorgeous doe eyes. "I have the option to leave it blank if you don't want me to."

"Please. Use my name. I'll be happy to be your reference." *Your friend. Your boyfriend. Whatever.*

"Thanks, buddy." He smiles and then goes back to filling out the paperwork.

I have the strongest urge to bring up what happened last night to try to clear the air. But hearing Martha and Sarah's words of advice replay in my head, I keep my mouth shut. If he isn't ready to talk about it, then I certainly am not going to mention it. I will give him whatever space and time he needs. At least he isn't asking me to leave.

"Done." He stands. "Wish me luck."

"Sure. For what?"

"That I can get a job in the cafeteria. Are you in a hurry?"

"I don't have to be anywhere until noon."

"Good. Let me turn this in and maybe I could trouble you with that tour around campus you offered me."

I'm so glad he's asking for my help. "I'll be happy to show you some shortcuts."

"You're a lifesaver. My sense of direction is shot. I wish you could have seen the look on my face when I walked into the women's locker room by mistake earlier. Why the door was unlocked I have no clue, but I could feel my cheeks burning when the girls started giggling and running for cover. I turned and walked out as fast as I could."

"You really do need my help. It took me a whole semester to figure out how to get around this place. But I'm surprised that you walked into the women's locker room. Isn't a good sense of direction necessary on the battlefield?" *Oh shit. Why did I bring that up?*

"It's easy on the battlefield. You just have to know where the bullets are coming from." He smiles, which makes me feel better. "I'm starving, how about you?"

"Famished."

"Breakfast is on me." He hands me a twenty-dollar bill. "The lady in charge asked me to fill this out today but won't be able to interview me until next week. Let me turn this application in and you order us some breakfast. Then we'll go on the tour. I'll be right back."

He walks away. His limp is gone. No one in the cafeteria has a clue that he is missing a leg but me. And it certainly doesn't bother me, not one bit. I don't know how he lost his leg, but obviously he hasn't quite accepted it yet. He mentioned a friend was supposed to help him initially, but the guy never showed. Did Adam have any help packing and loading before driving to Mockingbird Place? He didn't seem overly tired that night, but he is a strong guy. A former-Marine. I guess he's not limping because he got some rest after unloading his things into Malcolm's old place. *No, Adam's place. Unit A is Adam's.*

I go and order two sausage egg cheese biscuits and orange juices for us. When I get back to our table, he is already there.

Adam looks up at me. "Breakfast is served?"

I place the tray on the table. "Yes, sir." I can't resist and salute Adam, instantly worrying I might be overstepping again. Thus far he's been very closed mouth about his military service. But he returns the salute with a devilish grin, easing my concerns.

We eat our breakfast, talking about everything except the main issue on my mind.

"I bet you're glad our complex has a pool," he says. "It's going to be very hot according to the weatherman for the next several days."

"Swimming actually helps to clear my head when I have something I need to work out. You like to swim?"

He shrugs. "I used to. Taking a drive is my way to clear my mind."

I brace myself, thinking we might be getting close to opening Pandora's box about what happened.

But as usual, Adam changes the subject. "Oliver, how about you show me the buildings where my classes are going to be first?"

"I would love to."

He hands me his schedule, and I realize the lid on the infamous box is not only shut tight, it is also locked with no sign of the key in sight. What is it going to take for Adam to explain his sudden and over-the-top reaction to me learning he lost his leg? And will I ever find out if he is gay or straight?

As we leave the cafeteria, he asks, "Do you know the guy who lives in Unit D? Long black hair. Blue eyes. Good looking. He invited me to a party tonight at his and his roommate's place."

"That's Trace. I'm going, too. In fact the whole complex should be there. It'll give you another chance to get to know everyone."

"The ones who helped us move my things were very nice, though the MMA fighter is a bit intense."

"Tony's that way, but I believe he's really a good guy underneath all his crap."

"I wasn't sure I would go, but now that I know you're going I will."

We had so much drama last night, and today he's acting like it never happened. Now Adam says he is only going to the party if I'm going. *Damn.* He confuses me so much. I sense now is not the time to confront him with what I'm feeling. But if not now, when? "I'm glad you're going, too."

We walk around campus, and I point out the iconic spots.

"That's Dallas Hall, the oldest building on campus."

"It's quite grand. I like the dome."

When we get to the building that has the last class on his list, he turns to me. "Thanks, buddy."

Buddy. There's that word again. But better to be called that than nothing. I did say I would settle for friendship, but can I really? The more time I spend with him the more my feelings get mixed up.

"No trouble, Adam. I enjoyed hanging out."

"Me, too. I would have been completely lost on my first day of classes if it hadn't been for you and your fantastic tour." He sighs. "I better get back to looking for a job."

"Do you plan on working the entire time you're in school?"

"Yeah. With the financial aid I'm getting I don't have to work, but I want to. It will give me extra spending money and will keep me busy."

I have a feeling that he likes keeping busy so he doesn't have to face bigger issues inside him. "You don't seem like you would be happy working in food service to me. Have you thought about doing something else?"

"Like what?"

"I know the guy who heads the campus police department, Chief Torres. He told me the other day he has two openings. I bet he'd love to hire you, especially with your military background."

"Right." Adam shakes his head. "A one-legged Marine would make such a great police officer."

I'm nervous to push him, but have to try. At least he's mentioning his service—*and missing leg*. It's a start. "Adam, I saw you unload that truck and move all those boxes and furniture into your place. You're strong and capable. You would definitely be an asset to Torres's department."

"You really think so?"

My cell rings. "I know so." I answer the call.

"Oliver, where are you?" Candy's voice sounds frantic.

49

"I'm at the engineering building."

"That's clear across campus. You're supposed to speak in two minutes."

"Oh crap. The time got away from me. I'll run. Stall if you have to."

"Hurry. Love ya."

"Love ya more." I turn to Adam. "Sorry, but I have to go. I've got a speech to give."

"I'd like to hear it."

"Then follow me."

We take off running. Adam doesn't miss a step.

When we arrive in front of Dallas Hall, we see the crowd of LGBT supporters waving banners and flags.

Candy is addressing them. "We feel like we should have an answer from the Supreme Court by Monday and maybe even as early as Friday."

Before heading to the microphone, I turn to Adam. "You didn't break a sweat. I'm winded and you're not. You will make a great police officer for the university."

He smiles. "I've got to get the job first."

"You will. Trust me."

Candy spots me. "Please welcome to the podium, Rainbow Student Coalition's President, Mr. Oliver Lancaster."

"President?" Adam seems impressed.

I nod and run my hand through my hair, trying to straighten it. "How do I look?"

"You look great, Mr. President."

I grin, a little taken aback by his compliment, and walk to the stage to give my speech.

"Thank you for coming out today to show your support for those who are still denied basic human rights." I look out at the crowd, but my eyes keep seeking Adam. He sits in the back, staring at me. "Around the world and even in parts of our great nation people are arrested, beaten, bullied, and even killed for just living in their own truth, their own identity. Lesbian, gay, bisexual, and transgender individuals do not want special treatment, they only want and deserve the same things promised all citizens in the United States Constitution—life, liberty, and the pursuit of happiness. The Supreme Court has the power to take us one step closer to this dream. Marriage Equality is a basic human right."

Applause erupts. I glance at Adam to see if he is clapping. He isn't, but he hasn't left, which gives me some hope.

"The LGBT community needs to expand to include others who suffer from the same bigotry, marginalization, and oppression. It is important to broaden our tent to welcome and embrace new people who self-identify differently than the majority into our coalition."

I pause to let my words sink in, knowing there are still those who aren't convinced we need to change. Melody and Ashley sit side by side on the front row. They are beautiful, wonderful women, both transgender. I hope my speech will move them. I'm confident our meeting after the rally will go well. I look one more time at Adam, wondering how he feels about the rally and my speech.

"As you know I have proposed that the letters 'Q' 'I' and 'A' be added to our charter in the fall. LGBTQIA. What do those letters stand for? Let me begin with the letters 'I' and 'A,' and leave the 'Q,' the most controversial letter, for last. The 'I' represents intersex individuals born with a reproductive or sexual anatomy or chromosomes that don't seem to fit the typical definitions of female or male. In years past, doctors would perform surgery on some of these beautiful people, forcing a sexual identity on them. I believe these amazing individuals have the right to make their own decisions about their bodies and their identities, whether they want to stay the same or be male or female."

One of our more enthusiastic members yells out, "That's telling us how it should be, Oliver."

A few others say "Amen."

"The letter A actually represents two important groups, asexual persons as well as allies of LGBTQIA people."

I feel my heart thudding in my chest as painful relics from my past resurface.

"Which brings me to 'Q,' also representing two groups. One is called 'Questioning,' those who are looking for an orientation or questioning their own because they don't identify as heterosexual." Not able to stop myself, I look straight at Adam. Our eyes lock. What is he thinking?

"Call the roll, Brother Oliver," the same flamboyant member shouts.

"The second group represented by the letter 'Q' is 'Gender Queer.' The simplest definition I can give you is a gender queer individual's gender identity is not fully defined as either male or female. But it is the word 'queer' that many of us have issues with. It's a word from my teenage years, as well as many of yours, that was shouted at us again and again. Many times the word came with only curses. Other times with punches. And for some of us, the word 'queer' was accompanied by horrors so awful they are difficult to talk about."

The crowd is quiet, seeming to hang on my every word.

"Back then that word was always meant to demean, demoralize, and to shame those of us who didn't conform to our abusers' worldview of what was right and wrong."

My eyes lock with Adam's. I want this speech to make a difference, but now, with him here, I want him to understand what I went through. *At least part of what I went through.*

"I grew up in Winters, Texas, a very small town with no role models, no LGBTQIA people to help me find my way through the dark. I was alone and without hope. The word 'queer' hurt me then. But I refuse to give the power of that word to those who would like us to return to the shadows of shame and the basements of bitterness. This is our time. Many scholars and activists have reclaimed the word. No one has an issue with terms like Queer Cinema, Queer Literature, Queer Music. It is our time to join our scholars and activists here in Texas beginning with our own coalition. I say with pride that I'm a gay man, a queer man who wants to live his life openly, freely, pursuing happiness. That's my dream for us. LGBTQIA. I know it's a mouthful, but an important mouthful. Say it with me please. LGBTQIA."

The crowd rises and begins chanting LGBTQIA over and over.

"LGBTQIA. LGBTQIA. LGBTQIA."

"Lesbian."

"Lesbian," the crowd repeats.

"Gay."

"Gay," they shout back.

"Bisexual." I love the rising volume that comes when they repeat each word. "Transgender. Questioning. Gender Queer. Intersex. Asexual. Allies."

"Allies!" The crowd screams.

"The American dream. Our American dream."

Everyone cheers. Even Melody and Ashley. *They understand now.*

When I turn to look at Adam, he's gone, his seat empty. My heart sinks. Have I lost him for good?

Chapter 6

As people come up to congratulate me on the speech, I anxiously continue to look around for Adam. When I spot him standing off to the side talking to Candy, I breathe a sigh of relief. He hasn't left.

The energy around me is electric. My speech seems to have had the impact I'd hoped for.

"That was quite moving, Oliver," Melody says, standing next to Ashley. "We look forward to discussing this with you. Where should we go?"

"Let's meet in the Coalition's office, but would you mind if we delay it thirty minutes? I have a friend I need to walk over to the campus police."

"Oh you do, do you?" Ashley has a wicked sense of humor. "Where is this friend of yours?"

"Behave," Melody scolds her. "Of course we can wait. We'll see you in thirty."

The two women walk away.

I shake hands with more people, doing my duty but anxious to get back to Adam. When I finish speaking with the last person, I rush to him. He is still talking to Candy.

"Here's the man of the hour," Adam says, pulling me in for a hug, which thrills me. "Damn, you certainly know how to give a speech, buddy."

"I try." *Buddy.* Damn it. First a hug and then that word. I'm sick of hearing it.

"Try? You had us in the palm of your hands." Adam slaps me on the back like we are football players who just won the championship, not two gay guys who are attracted to each other. Or at least one gay guy attracted to the other guy, who might be gay or might be straight. My head is spinning.

Candy smiles. "He's right. You were incredible. You *are* incredible."

"I appreciate you saying that."

"Adam and I are getting to know each other," she says. "We have so much in common, like our service in the Marines and where we grew up. You never told me your friend is from Missouri. He grew up just outside of St. Louis and I'm from Springfield."

"I didn't know that." I'm glad to learn a little more about him. "Candy, you know that Adam and I just met."

"But we are friends," Adam adds. "In fact, very good friends."

What the hell does he mean by that? *Damn it.* He is killing me with his mixed messages. "Candy, I moved our meeting with Melody and Ashley back thirty minutes."

"How come?"

"I want to introduce Adam to Chief Torres. Adam is looking for a job and I think he would make a great campus police officer."

Her eyes light up. "I agree. He would be perfect. I know he and the chief will hit it off. Torres served in the Marines, too."

"Then he is a good guy," Adam says.

"He is a great guy, great man." I have built a close friendship with Chief Torres.

When his son came out to him and his wife a year ago, the Chief asked for my advice.

"OLIVER, I don't want to blow it with my son. What do I need to do?"

56

I tell him what I wished my parents had done for me. "Just accept him. Be yourself. Listen. That's all. The only thing that's changed is you found out he likes men. Big deal. He's still your son."

"You're absolutely right. I'm worrying for nothing. Instead of having a daughter-in-law some day, I'll get another son."

I TURN TO ADAM. "You ready to meet the chief?"

"Lead the way."

When we walk into the campus police headquarters, one of the officers sitting behind a desk looks up at us. "How may I help you?"

"We'd like to speak with Chief Torres," I tell her. "Would you let him know Oliver Lancaster is here?"

She stands and goes to the back.

I turn to Adam. "You really will like working here. The chief is good to his officers."

"Let me land a job first before we get the cart before the horse, Oliver," he says, reminding me of what Martha had said last night.

A minute later, Chief Torres comes out and greets us.

"Chief, this is a friend of mine, Adam Stockton, a former Marine."

The chief's eyes light up and he grabs Adam's hand. "Glad to meet you."

"Same here, Chief."

Candy was so right, as it is very clear the two guys have instantly hit it off.

"He's looking for a job." I look at the time on my phone, realizing I only have fifteen minutes to make my appointment. "And I heard you have a couple of openings in the department."

"I sure do, Oliver." The chief pats Adam on the back. "I definitely could use a man like you."

"There's something I need to tell you first, sir, before you make that decision." Adam's tone lowers. He clearly wants to limit anyone else learning about his missing leg. "Is there some place we could speak in private?"

"We can use my office."

"Chief, I've got a meeting I must get to, so I'm leaving Adam in your very capable hands."

"I'll take good care of him."

We shake hands, and I look at Adam. "I'll see you back at Mockingbird Place."

"It's a date."

A date? God, I couldn't be more confused. *Damn.*

Adam smiles, making me melt inside. "Thanks for introducing me to Chief Torres, Oliver. See you tonight at Trace's party."

I HELP Jackson put the finishing touches on the table for his and Trace's party. Trace links his phone to the speakers to play the music.

"Looks great, Jackson," I say.

Jackson steps back and inspects our work. "It's not quite right yet. We need to place the napkins and plates on both sides of the table, and they should match exactly."

I grin, realizing he is even more OCD than me. "You're right."

Jackson has that all-American, guy-next-door look. Thick light-brown hair that is never out of place, dark-blue eyes that mesmerize any onlookers, and a broad smile that invites people closer. As the star tennis player at the university, Jackson has absolutely no body fat. He is six-feet of lean, ripped muscles.

As we rearrange the table, I ask, "How's the new coach?"

"Don't know yet. He's still in Los Angeles." Jackson's former coach retired last year. "The guy sent the team an email this morning. He won't be in Dallas until Tuesday next week. I have heard through the grapevine that he can be a real asshole."

"But his team and its members win championships." Trace steps next to Jackson. "Give the new coach a chance. He's helped several men and women make the Olympics, and one even brought back the gold in 2012. And with your talent, you're going to be his next big success."

"I hope you're right." Jackson takes another glance at the table.

"That's perfect." He looks at his phone. "And just in time. Everyone will be arriving any minute."

Tugging slightly on the tablecloth, Trace winks at me. "That tablecloth doesn't look right to me, does it to you, Oliver?"

"What's wrong with it?" Jackson bends down to get a better look. "I see it now. You're right, Trace. It's hanging a quarter inch more on this side than the other."

Jackson straightens the tablecloth one more time. He isn't going to relax until the party is rocking.

Trace grins mischeviously and moves one of the trays that Jackson just placed a half-inch. "This is going to be a blast."

"Let's hope so." Jackson notices the plate's incorrect position and pushes it back to its original position.

Trace busts out laughing.

Jackson shakes his head and smiles. "Oh. I get you now, Trace Cotton. Just wait until the next spider shows up. You're on your own. And it will show up, especially the way you keep your room. What a mess. Lots of places for those creepy arachnids to hide."

"Don't be mean," Trace says. "My room has a comfy vibe."

Jackson smiles. There is a brotherly bond between these two that is easy to see. "Is that why you never make your bed?"

I shake my head. "You two are like Oscar and Felix."

The doorbell buzzes. Jackson and Trace go to welcome their first guest.

I hope Adam is at the door. I haven't been able to stop thinking about him since I left him with Chief Torres.

Jackson opens the door, and I'm happy to see it is Adam.

He holds a bottle of wine and a six-pack of beer. "I didn't know what to bring."

"These are perfect, Adam." Trace takes the gifts and leads him inside.

"Are you all settled into your new place?" Jackson asks.

"Some, but I still have a bunch of boxes to go through." He looks straight at me and smiles. "And don't forget, you, Mr. Lancaster, promised to help me decorate the place."

I nod, trying to accept the fact that I'm going to remain in a state of confusion when it comes to Adam.

"You picked a guy with an incredible eye for style," Jackson says.

The doorbell rings again.

As Trace and Jackson go back to greet their other guests, I turn to Adam. "How did it go with Chief Torres?"

And once again, he hugs me. "It went great. He wants me to start tomorrow."

"Tomorrow? Doesn't the department have to run a background check on you first?"

"Yes, but he says since you vouched for me, since I'm a former Marine, and since I gave him my application to the university and acceptance letter—I should be approved quickly. So he is having me come in for orientation first thing in the morning. But I won't be officially on the job until the background check is complete." Adam leans in close to me and in a very low tone says, "You were right. He didn't give a damn about my leg."

I whisper, "I knew he wouldn't care."

What a difference there is in Adam since I first learned about his missing leg. Now he seems to trust me with his secret. *At least the secret about his leg.*

"I need a drink, buddy. Where's the bar?"

Buddy. And just like that, I feel his walls go back up. "Kitchen. I'll show you."

When we go back into the living room with our drinks, the party is in full swing. Everyone from the complex, except Jaris the doctor and Eli the fireman, is here. Our resident musical trio walks in the door together. Josh and Franki carry their guitars and Chad enters with his portable keyboard. All three of them are dressed in wild colors, but Chad, the leader of the group and the most flamboyant has on a large pink top hat with a matching boa around his neck. Josh has on green leather pants and a purple shirt. Franki sports a tie-dye T-shirt and jeans. Her black hair is spiked.

Chad hugs Trace. "Sorry we're late."

"Don't worry about it," Trace says. "I'm just glad you could make it. We cleared a space by the sofa for the three of you to set up."

"This is the trio everyone's been telling me about?" Adam asks me.

"Yes it is. They really are amazing musicians. Get ready though. Whenever they play at our parties they ask each of us to sing a song."

He smiles. "What if I don't know any of their songs?"

"Not to worry. They can play anything."

"Hey everyone," Jackson says. "I'd like for you to bring your attention to our friends from Unit G—Chad, Josh, and Franki, the trio known as Red Shimmer."

The group claps as the trio begins performing a fast-paced song. Martha grabs Sarah and they start dancing. Most join them, including me, lost to the magic the trio is creating through their music. Tony doesn't, which is no surprise. He never does. Adam also remains standing to the side, but unlike Tony, he is smiling, apparently enjoying himself. And then it hits me like a ton of bricks why Adam might not be dancing. *His prosthetic leg.*

Concerned he might be feeling uncomfortable, I stop dancing and move next to him. "So? What do you think of Red Shimmer?"

"My God, they are good. They should have a record deal."

"I agree. They signed with one a year ago but it was a shady outfit that went bankrupt before any of their songs could be released. They've put out some tracks on iTunes themselves, and they're working to get a new deal with a more legitimate record company." I sit down on the floor to watch the rest of their set, leaning back against the wall.

"Refill?" Adam holds up his empty bottle.

"Yes. Please." I hand him mine.

Adam goes into the kitchen.

Tony takes a step my direction and looks down on me. "You may be barking up the wrong tree, Oliver."

"What do you mean by that?"

"You know what I mean. Adam. The Marine."

"You and I are friends, Tony, but that's none of your business."

"Friends? You and I? I guess. Why not?" And in typical Tony fashion, whenever things get too real for him, he moves away, this time to the other side of the room.

Adam comes back with two beers and hands me one.

"Thanks."

He smiles and sits down on the floor next to me. I'm very pleased.

"Time to hear your lovely voices." Chad turns to Martha and Sarah. "You're up to bat, ladies."

Gazing into each other's eyes, the two women sing a beautiful love song from the 50s.

I'm always amazed at how in love with each other they still are after so many years.

"Oliver, you were right." Adam leans in close, so close the urge to kiss him feels unbearable. "The band *can* play anything. They're fantastic, and Martha and Sarah can really sing, too."

"You'll have to hear Martha and Sarah's story about how they met in high school choir."

"Really? That long ago? Good for them."

"They've known each other since they were ten years old. Their birthdays are just three days apart." I take a sip of beer. "Anyway, when you have a little time, go over to their place so they can tell you their story. They love to talk about it and it's worth hearing."

"I definitely will."

"Who's next?" Chad asks, his gaze landing on Adam. "New guy. How about you?"

It surprises me when Adam stands.

"I'll do my best, but Martha and Sarah are a tough act to follow." Adam shakes each of the trio's hands and introduces himself. Then he asks them to play a hit song by K-5 Checkmate.

"Wow," Lashaya said. "I love them."

"Should I be jealous, baby?" Hayden teases.

"Don't be silly," she says.

"Key of F, guys," Adam tells the trio.

I'm excited to hear him sing. Whether he has any talent like Martha and Sarah, or if he can't stay on key to save his life, like me, doesn't matter. I'm about to learn more about him and that makes me happy.

But when he starts singing, everyone holds their breaths, including me. Adam's voice is amazing, like an angel. Chad and Josh start singing the backup harmonies.

When the song ends, we shout, "Encore. Encore."

Our reaction seems to surprise Adam. "Are you serious?"

Franki laughs. "I believe they are. Come on, Adam. Sing another one."

The group applauds.

And without waiting for him to consent, the trio begins playing another K-5 Checkmate song.

"Come on, Adam," Chad coaxes. "We can't let your fans down, and I'm sure you know this song too."

"If you really want me to," he says and starts singing with the band.

My heart melts.

He looks straight at me when he sings the line *"Finding you changed my life."*

Damn. *Is he or isn't he?* The question keeps rolling around in my mind, driving me crazy. I've experienced how Adam can be open about so many things. But on topics that hit his buttons, he can shut down in a split second. Hot and cold. On and off.

Am I misinterpreting his actions toward me? Maybe it isn't flirting at all. Maybe he is just teasing me. But isn't teasing a type of flirting? I sigh, feeling more confused than ever. I know one way to find out is when the song ends to get up and plant a big kiss on him. Then he'd have to admit one way or the other how he feels about me. I smile to myself, knowing I won't take that chance. At least for now we are friends.

At the end of the number, cheers go up for Adam.

"Thank you but no more. Someone else needs to sing." Adam points at me. "How about you, Oliver?"

"I would but I don't want the party to end. How about you, Tony?"

"Not me. I wouldn't follow such a stellar performance by *your*

Marine." Tony looks Adam in the eyes. "I never would have taken you for a fan of boy bands like K-5. So the question that has been on all our minds is answered."

"What question?" Adam asks.

"You're gay. Right?"

Adam's face darkens but he doesn't answer.

Fearless, as always, Chad jumps in front of Tony. "What's the matter with you? How rude. We don't give a damn if he's gay or straight or asexual or bi or whatever. He's our new friend."

Tony looks at me, and I realize he only pushed the issue with Adam because in his mind it will help me. How Tony knows what I feel for Adam is a mystery to me. Or am I just that transparent?

"It's time for me to go." The angry MMA fighter marches to the door.

"That's not what any of us want, Tony," Chad says. "Just go sit down and try to have a good time."

But Tony walks out the door, slamming it behind him.

Chad shakes his head. "I tried, guys."

"Yes, you did," Martha says. "Give Tony some space."

"Sure, but until he starts acting like a normal human being, I'm not going to let him ruin this party." Chad smiles at me. "Hey, Oliver. How about a rousing round of 'Row, Row, Row, Your Boat'?"

"Not a chance," I answer, concerned about how Tony's outburst has impacted Adam. "You sing something. You're the professional."

"I thought you'd never ask."

The trio starts playing one of their most upbeat songs, lightening everyone's mood. Then I look at Adam and can see his mood is stormy and dark. Tony's question obviously is still bothering him even though the MMA fighter has already left.

Adam downs his beer and then steps over to Trace and Jackson. "Thanks for a wonderful time. I really enjoyed myself."

I don't want him to leave but I'm not surprised he wants to.

"Adam, you're not going now, are you?" Trace asks. "The party is just getting going."

"I start my new job at the campus police station in the morning. I want to get plenty of sleep."

"We're very glad you came," Jackson says. "Someone in the complex is always hosting a party, so you'll have a lot of other events to get to know us all better. In fact, if the Supreme Court announces their ruling tomorrow, we're going to celebrate with a barbeque and pool party."

"What if it doesn't go your way?" Adam asks.

"Well, we're still planning on getting together either way," Trace says. "We'll eat, drink and swim. Martha and Sarah provide all the meat. Everyone brings a side dish or dessert, but since you're our newest neighbor you just need to bring your swimsuit."

"Not much of swimmer, but I'll be there." Adam leaves without saying goodbye to me—*or even looking at me.*

I think about chasing after him, but feel like I might be the last person he wants to see right now. It crushes me. Are Tony's good intentions going to ruin things for me with Adam? Maybe we don't have a chance at being more than friends. I want to be his friend at least. *Buddies.* But if I'm honest with myself, I want so much more.

"You look like you could use another drink, Oliver." Jackson hands me a fresh beer.

"Thanks."

"You alright?"

"Only processing what just happened. Adam isn't the kind of guy you push like Tony tried to do." I recall Adam's reaction to me seeing the prosthetics in his closet. "He's private about some things. He needs his space."

"That doesn't sound like you, Oliver." Jackson takes a sip of his beer. "You're the guy who seduces men out of the closet. I remember you saying to me not that long ago that you didn't believe in secrets."

"I don't, but Adam is different. And I don't even know if he's gay or not. What I do know is I want to be his friend."

"Who do you think you're kidding?" Jackson smiles. "You want much more than that. You couldn't take your eyes off of him the whole time he was here."

Chad walks up holding his giant glass that he brings to every party. Hanging from the rim are three paper umbrellas. "Am I interrupting?"

"Not at all," Jackson says. "Our boy Oliver needs some cheering up, and who better than you for the job."

He spreads his arms wide and turns to me. "Tell your sister Chad what's wrong."

I can't help but smile. Chad has that way with people. "I'm very confused when it comes to our new neighbor."

I tell Chad what has happened so far between Adam and me, holding back only one detail. *Adam's missing leg.* I made a promise and mean to keep it.

"Oh, honey, the boy is gay. It's obvious. He just has some things to work out. And besides, aren't you the expert at helping men out of the closet. What was the name of the last one you dated?"

"Trent," I answer.

"Yes. Trent. Cute. He's down at the bars now dancing until closing. I remember when you took him to one of our gigs. First time he'd ever been in a gay bar. He looked like a little scared puppy." Chad hugs me and kisses my cheek. "Just work your magic on Adam, Oliver."

"It's different with Adam."

"Now I get it, Mr. Lancaster." Chad grins. "I think you might be falling in love."

"I know I like him. I like him very much."

"Okay, then, let me help you with this one. Send him flowers. It'll be clear that you're interested in being more than friends but it won't be so overt to push him away if Adam turns out to be straight."

"Or if he's gay and not interested in me."

"Like there's any chance of that, you adorable man. I know Adam is gay and I'll bet he's into you, too." Chad turns to Jackson. "Did you see how Adam kept staring at our boy when he was singing?"

"I sure did."

"You both saw that too? I wasn't just imagining it?"

66

"Of course you weren't," Chad answers. "The rest of us were invisible to you and Adam during his two songs. All either of you could see was each other."

I begin to hope that Chad might be right, that things are going to be okay between Adam and me.

"And it wasn't just Chad and I who noticed." Jackson puts his hand on my shoulder. "Everyone, including Tony, saw it. That's why I think Tony did what he did."

"Me, too," I say. "Tony is…well, he's…difficult to understand, but I think under all that sarcasm and anger is a good man."

"It's going to take a very special guy to get past all Tony's crap," Chad says. "But you know me. I'm the ultimate optimist. Everyone has someone out there. Even Tony. Even me. But back to you and Adam. Are you going to take my brilliant advice and send that sexy ex-Marine flowers?"

I smile. "It's *former* Marine he told me."

"Former. Ex. I'm focused on one word and you should be too. Sexy. I think roses would be nice."

"Cupid, put your arrows away," I say with a grin. "I'll think about it."

Chapter 7

It is twenty minutes past one in the morning. Trace and Jackson's party is still going strong. I leave early to get ready for my late-night swim to clear my head.

I send a text to Candy. *You awake?*

I'm now. LOL!

Sorry. Can I call you? I need to talk.

Of course, she texts back.

I call her number.

"What's wrong, Oliver?"

"I guess, I'm just a little confused about Adam." I tell her what happened at the party with Tony confronting him.

"Honey, it's going to be fine. Adam has issues like most of us do. You're really into him, aren't you? This sounds more serious than I've ever heard you talk about anyone else before. Even Trent."

"I don't know. I guess so. Maybe it's a mistake to pursue this. We just buried Malcolm. My emotions are all mixed up about everything."

"No one is expecting you to get married. Just take one step at a time and be patient. If it's meant to be, it will work out."

"You're right, sis." I smile. "Thanks. Love ya."

"Love ya more."

Wearing my swimming trunks, I grab a towel and walk out of my apartment.

Before I dive into the pool, I spot Adam sitting on his steps. He stands and walks over to me.

"Hey," he says in that deep, sexy tone of his that drives me wild. "Is the party still going?"

I nod. "I'm surprised you're up so late. I thought you had to report to the new job early."

"I do. Seven-thirty. Couldn't sleep though. We need to talk."

I'm shocked to hear him say that and a little concerned. Is Adam about to tell me to shove off? That he doesn't want to be friends any more? I can't blame him, especially after what happened with Tony.

"Adam, I'm sorry about Tony. He doesn't know when to keep his mouth shut."

"He just threw me for a loop, Oliver. But this isn't about Tony or even what he said. This is about you and me. Well, really it's about me—what I need to tell you about myself." He points at the bench next to Malcolm's tree. "Let's sit down."

As we walk over to the bench, I notice him clenching his hands. I can feel his apprehension. What is so terrible that has this war hero so uneasy?

We sit side by side without either of us saying a word. Each second feels like an eternity to me, but I wait for him to speak first.

He sighs. "Where to begin? Damn. This is harder than I thought it would be."

"Take your time. There's no rush. I'm here, Adam." I hope he trusts me, trusts me enough to share *his truth*. "If it takes all night, I'll be here."

He smiles weakly. "You're not like anyone I've ever met before, Oliver."

"I hope that's a good thing," I say with a smile, trying to lessen the tension.

"I owe you an apology."

"For what?" I ask. "I thought we had a good time at the party."

"We did. You were great. It's not about that. It's about me treating you like crap at my place when you saw my prosthetics." His eyes never leave mine. "I'm very sorry how I acted."

"It's okay."

"No, it's not okay. I was an ass. You've been nothing but kind to me."

"I can't imagine how you feel, what you've been through."

Another sigh leaves his lips, this one filled with pain and regret. "I've been to counseling, and most of the time I'm fine with it. I just don't like people knowing."

"Your secret is safe with me."

"I already know it is. Not one person mentioned it at the party. And when I didn't join in on the dancing, you stopped and came over to me. I know why. It was your way of rescuing me. You didn't want me to stick out, to feel different. Thank you for that. You know I can dance, walk, run. All the things I used to do with two legs. I have different prosthetics for different tasks, thanks to my Grand-dad's generosity. But now, when I'm tired I limp and people notice. I don't want to be noticed for not having a leg. I don't want sympathy or pity. I just want to be normal. Like everyone else."

His walls are down. I feel close to him. Safe. Does he feel safe with me? I have to know.

"Adam, do you mind me asking how you lost your leg?"

"I don't mind at all. The counselor has told me that talking about it is a good thing for me, but you're the first person I've ever wanted to share it with."

I'm in awe that he trusts me this much.

He turns and stares at the surface of the pool, which reflects the moon above us and the shimmering lights of the complex's lampposts dancing on the water. "I was in Afghanistan, only six months into my second tour of duty when it happened. Three of my fellow Marines and me were in a lead Humvee of a caravan transporting a civilian news team to another base when we hit an IED. The explosion flipped the vehicle, and threw me out, crushing my leg. I don't know how long I was out for. A few seconds. But when I came to, I knew we were in trouble. The

Humvee was on fire and my buddies were still inside, obviously unconscious."

"Oh my God, Adam."

"The pain was so intense it almost made me pass out. But I willed myself to keep moving, to stay focused, and to use my training. I don't know how I was able to get them out, but I did, crawling on the ground inch by inch without the use of my injured leg, gunfire all around. When I got them out, the Humvee exploded. A moment later, I succumbed to the pain and lost consciousness. When I came to a week later, I learned the doctors had to take my leg. Turned out a medic saved my life. She'd put a tourniquet on me moments after I passed out. The other Marines in the caravan engaged the enemy while I was pulling out my friends. We were lucky that day. No one died. Everyone survived."

I was in awe of him. "Those men would have died if you hadn't pulled them out. You're a hero, Adam."

"I'm no hero. I was a Marine just doing my job." He looked at me with his big dark eyes. "They would have done the same for me."

"Adam, I don't know what to say. I just...I can't imagine... how..." Overcome with emotion and with tears falling from my eyes, I wrap my arms around him. "You're wrong. You *are* a hero."

I hold onto him tight.

Then he hugs me back.

We remain in each other's arms for several moments.

"You get me, Oliver." He leans back, keeping hold of me. Our eyes lock on each other. And then to my surprise, he presses his lips to mine.

We hear a door open and Adam releases me.

I turn and see everyone at Trace and Jackson's party streaming out of their unit.

Adam stands and walks back to his apartment without even saying goodbye. I hate that we were interrupted and that his guard is back up. We were just getting real. *Damn. One step forward, two steps back.*

I think about chasing after him, but I'm worried that will draw attention to him from the others. I know Adam isn't ready to face them.

As I watch him shut his door, a million thoughts swirl in my head. He saved those men. He deserves to be happy, to live in his truth. Why is he in the closet? What shame does he carry?

Sarah and Martha are the only ones who spot me. The rest enter their homes, leaving the three of us in the courtyard.

"Looks like your midnight swim is getting later and later," Martha says, puffing on a cigarette. "You do realize it's two am?"

I want to tell them what happened with Adam, that he kissed me, but I know that would be breaking his confidence. So instead, I say, "It's that late? I promise I won't splash too loud."

They laugh and disappear into their unit.

I dive into the pool, swimming to the other side.

Adam kissed me, and that changes everything. He is gay—or bi or curious. I want to learn more about his truth, a truth that he is clearly running away from.

I swim more laps, but my thoughts won't settle down.

I know he is too good for me. God, what I would give if we could have a fairy tale's happily ever after. But I have too much baggage. I'm in deeper than I thought was possible. But in spite of that, I vow I will help him embrace who he really is. A month. Two months. However long it takes. Getting any closer to him will just end up breaking my heart, but I don't have a choice. He's a hero that needs to be rescued.

Chapter 8

Even though it is already past lunchtime, I'm still in my robe, sitting on my patio drinking coffee. After tossing and turning all night long, I finally got up early this morning to make the potato salad for the barbeque. I can't stop thinking about the kiss. *Adam's kiss.*

Adam told me I wasn't like anyone he'd ever met before. He's right, but not the way he thinks. I grimace as a dark memory from my first few months in Dallas resurfaces in my mind in sharp focus. I hate secrets, but that time in my life is a secret I must keep. Even from Adam. *Especially from Adam.*

He isn't like anyone I've ever known either. Very mysterious. Very guarded. Very very sexy. And to top everything off, Adam is a hero. He actually saved lives.

I'm not even in his league, especially with my history. Malcolm was the only one who knew my deep, dark secret. Not even Candy knows what happened back then. I've thought about telling her so many times, but I just can't face her being disappointed in me.

Malcolm took my secret to his grave.

Even if I don't have a chance to be with Adam, I still want to help him. It's obvious that he's not comfortable with his sexuality.

Hell, he denied being gay the day we met. And yet he kissed me. I can help him out of the closet. I've done it for others. Like Trent. I can do it for Adam too. I'm risking my heart, but I must.

I need to get my mind on something else, so I turn on my iPad to check Facebook and catch up on the news. The first thing I read blows me away.

Supreme Court Rules In Favor of Same-Sex Marriage!

"They actually did it." My eyes tear up.

A five-four decision. Marriage Equality is now the law of the land.

I grab my phone. There are twenty-five texts and five voicemail messages, three from Candy. "I turned the ringer off last night."

I bet everyone is already partying. I wish Malcolm had lived to see this day. The first person I must call is Candy.

She answers, full of excitement, "We won, Oliver. We actually won."

"I know. It's so unreal. You have to come to the barbeque to celebrate."

"I would but I think the coalition needs to have a parade on Sunday and I'm already gathering the troops to get things underway. I got permission from President Anderson to hang rainbow flags all over the campus."

"You're too much. You love organizing parties, rallies, and parades. How do you do it? When do you sleep, Candy?"

"I'll grab a few hours when I can this weekend. Oliver, we just witnessed history. Sleep is the last thing on my mind."

"You're right about that, sis. I can drop off my potato salad for the barbeque and then I can meet you."

"No. I've got this. You've been through so much. Celebrate with your friends at Mockingbird Place. You and I can talk tomorrow. Besides, I can use your help then. And you might ask Adam if he wants to help, too."

"Trying to play Cupid?"

"Guilty." She laughs. "Love ya."

"Love ya more."

A loud banging on my front door startles me.

76

I rush to the door, ready to hug whoever wants to celebrate.

"Hold on. I'm coming."

I open the door and find a very angry Adam, wearing a campus police uniform and holding a dozen yellow roses.

He shoves the flowers into my chest. "What the hell were you thinking sending these to me at the station on my very first day?"

His words sting me. I ordered the roses online in the early morning hours. "I thought I was being nice."

"Nice? Hell. All you did was embarrass me." He tosses the flowers to the floor, turns around, and storms off.

"Wait." I pick the flowers up. "Let's talk about this, Adam."

"I don't want to talk, and I don't have time to talk. This is my lunch break. I have to get back to work."

"Can we talk later?"

He doesn't respond but continues his indignant march to the parking lot.

When he is out of sight, I go back inside and close the door. I'm devastated.

"Fuck." I look at the flowers in my hand. I was an idiot to order them.

I should have given it more thought. I shouldn't have sent the damn roses. I should have known he wasn't ready. Yes, he kissed me. But it was only one kiss. The moment everyone started filing out of Trace and Jackson's apartment last night, he left me on the bench without saying a word.

How many clues do I need to figure out how private a person Adam is? Is there any way I can fix this? Maybe not, but I do know that I can at least get his apartment set up for his mom like he asked me to. It is the one thing I can do and not mess up.

I get dressed and go to Martha and Sarah's place.

Martha opens the door and hugs me. "Can you believe it? We won. The Supremes did the right thing. Now Sarah and I can get married in Texas and so can you and Adam."

"That's wonderful for you and Sarah, but don't get the cart before the horse concerning me and Adam, Martha."

"I know. I know. I'm just so happy."

"It is a wonderful day that none of us will ever forget." But my mind isn't on the court's decision. It's the look on Adam's face when he shoved the roses into my chest that I can't stop thinking about.

"Sarah was about to make us some lunch. Would you like to join us?"

"No thanks. I'm actually in a rush. I want to get Adam's apartment set up for him before he comes home from his new job."

"Oh, yes. I heard him at the party talking about you decorating the unit for him." Martha steps outside, lights a cigarette, and calls back into the apartment. "S, can you bring the key to Unit A out here for me?"

From inside Sarah answers, "M, I'll be right there."

I'm trying to appear casual, to not let on that I'm dying inside. I wish I had time to talk to these two wonderful women and get their advice, but there's no time. So I put on a false smile, a trick I learned in my previous life in Dallas, to give the illusion everything is just fine.

"So what ideas do you have for his place?" Martha asks me.

"Not sure yet. I need to see what he has for art and decorations. That will be my starting point."

"That's a good idea, but from what I saw of his things when we were moving him in—there isn't much. A few posters and family photos. There might be more in all those boxes though."

Please hurry, Sarah. Bring the key. "I'm certain there will be plenty."

"Are you okay?" Martha asks, her eyes narrowing.

"Yes. I'm fine." I hate to lie to her but what other choice do I have.

Sarah joins us on the steps, holding the key to Unit A. "Where's Adam?"

"At the university," I tell her. "Today is his first day on the job for the campus police. May I have his key, please?"

"The key is for you then?"

I nod and hold out my hand.

She doesn't give me the key. "This is a little unusual, Oliver. Adam didn't give us permission to give you his key yet."

"Oh, S." Martha puts her arms around Sarah. "Such a stickler for rules. Don't you remember Adam saying at the party last night that Oliver was going to decorate his place for him?"

"But—"

"But nothing. You're the one who says these two belong together. Oliver is just trying to do something nice for Adam." Martha turns to me. "This is a surprise for him, right?"

"Yes, it is." At least that isn't a lie. But holding back details isn't something I normally do with them. As uncomfortable as it makes me feel, it's what I have to do right now. I need that key.

"Look at our sweet Oliver, S. He just wants to do something nice for Adam. Are you going to stand in the way of young love?"

Sarah smiles and kisses Martha. "I never win with you, sweetheart. Fine." She hands me the key. "Here, Oliver. Go do your best."

"I'll try. Thank you." I look at the time on my phone and realize I have to hurry if I'm going to finish before Adam returns. "I'll bring the key back before the barbeque gets started."

Sarah lights her cigarette. "Don't forget, you're bringing your delicious potato salad for the party."

"I won't forget. Made it early this morning." I say my goodbyes and walk over to Unit A.

I unlock the door and enter Adam's place. As fast as I can, I unpack his boxes, finding a very eclectic collection—pieces from all parts of the world. A wooden box from Spain. A brass table from Morocco. A painting of the Eifel Tower. The Marine flag. A poster of a rock band. And more. At the moment, I'm unsure how I'm going to make them all work as a group. But the longer I work on his place, the more I get a sense of how his pieces can fit together.

It takes me no time to get his kitchen set up. He doesn't have many dishes and only one skillet and one pot—the same pot we'd eaten the Ramen noodles out of that first night.

God, I hope what I'm doing will be enough for Adam to forgive me for sending the flowers to the station.

Quickly, I move furniture, put up artwork, and arrange shelves. I come to the last box, which is marked "Family Framed Photos." I know the perfect place for them, the Indonesian table that I'd placed by his front window.

The first picture I see is of a woman in a white dress and Adam in his Marine uniform. God, he is so handsome. I guess she is his mother. The next is of him at his high school graduation in cap and gown, with the same woman next to him smiling broadly. Where is his father?

Another is of Adam standing in front of a building with three other Marines. Was this taken in Afghanistan? Before the caravan was bombed? Before Adam lost his leg? Were the men in the picture with him the ones he saved?

The final photo I find is of a much younger version of the woman, pregnant and standing by another Marine. Is this Adam's father? The man has the same dark eyes as Adam.

There are so many questions about Adam I have. I wish I could find the answers.

I take all the empty boxes to the dumpster, sweep and mop the floors, and dust every surface. When I'm done, I look around at my work. The place is fantastic. It suits Adam. And then an idea hits me.

Glancing at the time on my phone, I know I have to hurry.

I run to my place and get the roses. Despite being tossed to the floor, they are in pretty good shape. I put them in a vase, grab a notepad and pen, and go back to Unit A. Placing the flowers on Adam's kitchen table, I jot down a message for him.

ADAM,

I'm so sorry I sent these to your work.

I was such a dumbass. I hope you will forgive me and enjoy them in your home.

Oliver

Chapter 9

Nervously looking for any sign of Adam at the barbeque in the courtyard, I carry the bowl of potato salad. I don't see him anywhere. Is he still at the campus?

Everyone else in the complex is here, even the doctor and fireman—Jaris and Eli. What an unexpected treat that they both could be here at the same time, especially with their crazy hours.

Franki is playing a solo on her guitar.

Trace and Jackson are getting the grill ready.

Martha and Sarah are hanging rainbow flags on the lampposts.

Tony sits in one of the chairs away from the group looking at his phone.

The rest are in the pool.

The mood is quite festive. Why wouldn't it be? Getting married to the one you love, no matter their gender, is the law now, even in conservative Texas.

I'm thrilled about the Supreme Court's decision this morning, but it's very difficult to be in a party mood when all I can think of is how pissed Adam looked when I opened my door.

Wearing rainbow-colored trunks, Chad comes up to me. "So? Where's your Marine? Did you send him flowers?"

My heart sinks. "I know you meant well, Chad, but the flowers turned out to be a mistake. He was pissed to the point that he came over and shoved them in my chest and left. I haven't seen him since. I don't know where we stand now."

"Oh my God, love. I'm so sorry. I thought it was a great idea."

"It's not your fault. I didn't have to send them, especially to his work."

"You sent them to his work?" Chad frowns. "Oh, honey, you shouldn't have done that."

"I'm quite aware of that now. Just call me a dumbass, with a capital D."

Chad puts his arm around me. "We're going to work on that boy and get him straightened out." He winks. "I mean *gayed*-out. Don't wave the white flag just yet."

"I'm trying not to, but it's difficult." I tell Chad about how I decorated Adam's place.

"Oh, Oliver. That's got to be the most romantic thing I've ever heard in my life."

"I left the roses on his kitchen table with a note saying I'm sorry. You think he'll be mad?"

"Let's just say if he is, he's a fool. You're a great guy, Oliver. Anyone would be lucky to date you." He looks past me. "Here comes *your* Marine now. Give me that bowl and go talk to him."

"No. I've pushed him enough. I need to let him come to me when he's ready." I look over my shoulder and see Adam talking to Sarah.

"Why is he wearing jeans?" Chad asks. "Didn't he know this was a pool party?"

"We probably forgot to tell him," I lie. I have a good idea what the real reason is, but I'm not about to betray Adam's confidence about his missing leg. "What I do know is this. It's his move, Chad."

"You're probably right. Let's get some drinks."

"I could use one."

I try to enjoy myself, but can't. As the time passes, I keep glancing at Adam, which only reminds me how we left things. Damn, I want to talk to him but know I can't.

"You've got to stop dwelling on him, Oliver," Chad says. "Dive into the pool. You're the one who says swimming clears your head."

"Chad, come on." Franki waves him over. "Martha and Sarah want us to sing."

He leans in close to me. "Don't give in yet. Adam will come to his senses. You'll see."

Chad joins the others next to the grill, where Red Shimmer has set up their equipment. Once they start playing, Martha and Sarah begin dancing, and Lashaya grabs Hayden's hand and joins them.

I finish my drink and sit on the edge of the pool, dangling my legs in the water. I wish Candy was here. She always knows what to say to cheer me up. But at the end of the day, I doubt even she would be able to turn my mood around.

When I look back at Adam, I see he's talking to Tony, smiling, and seems to be having a good time.

Why is he avoiding me? It's probably because he's still angry with me about the flowers.

He has to have seen how I decorated his place when he went home to change out of his uniform. Can it be that he doesn't like how I set it up? And what about my note? How does he feel about that?

Normally, I'm able to sense what people are thinking, but with Adam I'm always confused.

Chad hands me a fresh drink. "Oliver, you need to try to relax. This is a party."

"I know it is, and I know I said it was Adam's move, but I'm about done waiting."

"Good luck," Chad says and then dives into the pool.

When I turn back Adam's direction and see him leading Tony into his place, my gut tightens. "Shit."

I down half of the contents of my glass. What the hell is going on? Is Adam into Tony? Why did he kiss me then? Damn it. It doesn't make sense. I'm more confused than ever. And angry. Martha and Sarah, even Chad believes Adam will come around. But I'm not so sure about that anymore after what I just saw.

I glance at the tree we planted for Malcolm. "What the hell

should I do?" A memory flashes in my mind to another party where I'd also been very angry.

MALCOLM COMES *up beside me and says, "I know what you're thinking, Oliver."*

"Do you?" I snap back. "That joke that jerk told wasn't funny."

"No, it wasn't, and I told him so. He's gone. I asked him to leave."

"Good. That creep has no idea what it's like to live on the streets."

"I know it struck a nerve with you." Malcolm puts his arm around my shoulders. "You did what you had to do to survive. Stop beating yourself up."

"I don't know how."

"You can start by coming back downstairs and enjoying the party with our friends. That will get your mind off of the past. And you might actually start having some fun."

I LOOK over at Malcolm's tree. "Thanks for the advice—again."

Trying to let go of my anger and forget that Adam and Tony are in Unit A together, I walk up to our resident fireman. "Hey Eli. How's it going?"

"Pretty good."

Eli is easy-going, except when it comes to his ex. That creep continues to screw Eli over. Martha and Sarah have encouraged Eli to start dating again, but he's made it clear to them and everyone else at the complex that he isn't interested in meeting anyone.

"Glad you could make it," I say.

"I'm on vacation for the next two weeks."

"That's cool." I glance back at Adam's front door, which remains shut. What are he and Tony doing in there? "Going anywhere?"

"I leave for Chicago tomorrow. I'll be visiting my sister and her family for a week. The week after, I'll be back here. I plan on chilling by the pool the whole time."

"That sounds like a plan." I see Adam's door open.

He and Tony walk out. Both are smiling.

As I continue talking to Eli, Adam leads Franki and Josh into his apartment. "What the hell is up with him?"

"With who?" Eli asks. "The Marine?"

"Yes."

"Adam something, right?"

"Adam Stockton." I've been at the party for over an hour and Adam still hasn't spoken to me. But he's talked to Tony and taken him inside his apartment. Jealousy rises inside me.

"I heard he's a nice guy, but do you have a problem with him?" Eli asks.

"I don't know, but I'm going to find out. Excuse me." I walk up to Adam's door, just as Franki and Josh walk out of Unit A, leaving the door open. Adam is not with them.

"Oh my God, Oliver," Franki says. "What you did…well, it is incredible."

"Incredible? I'm confused."

"Adam's apartment is stunning."

Josh nods. "You need to come to our place and give us some tips on how to decorate."

"So that's why he was taking you inside. And Tony. He was showing you how I decorated the place?"

"Why else, Silly?" Franki hugs me. "You are so talented. Adam loves everything you did."

Not everything. Not the flowers.

"He even made us take our shoes off because it's so clean," Josh says.

"He really likes it? He hasn't told me." I'm pissed.

I still don't know how he feels about me. Yeah, he is happy that his apartment is put together, but he hasn't said a single word to me since shoving the flowers in my chest. I'm done waiting.

It is time to confront him, no matter the outcome. "Where is Adam?"

"Inside. His mother called and he's talking to her," Josh says. "Franki, Chad is motioning for us to play another set."

"We better go then."

The two of them leave and I walk into Unit A.

Holding his cell, Adam stands in the kitchen with his back to me.

I sit down in a chair so he will see me the moment he turns around.

"Mom, I love it here. All the people are so nice. I can't wait for you to see my place. My friend Oliver decorated it for me. It looks amazing."

I'm pleased that he likes what I have done but am still upset that he hasn't told me.

"No. I didn't serve with him. He's a student at the college. When do you think you'll be here?" He turns around and our eyes lock. "Mom, that works great. Be safe driving. I'll see you soon. I love you, too." He puts his phone away. "Hi."

"Hi? Really? That's all you have to say to me?"

"Uh. Thank you."

"You've got to be kidding. I can't take any more of this." I stand, walking to the door.

Adam comes up behind me and puts his arms around me. "Don't go. I just didn't know what to say. My place is so beautiful. No one has ever done anything like this for me. And I really love the flowers. I'm sorry for being such a jerk. Again."

I twist free of his hold, turn and face him. "That's just it, Adam. You're up and down too much. Hot and cold. This—whatever *this* is —isn't for me." I walk to his front door and step out of Unit A.

"Oliver, wait. Can we please just talk?"

"What good would that do, Adam?" The best I can hope for with him is two, maybe three months. Best to end it before it begins and save myself some heartache. "I can't wait and I don't want to talk. I'm done."

I march to my place, not ready to join the others at the pool party. I know if I turn around and face Adam, my willpower will crumble. One more look into his dark, sexy eyes and I'll forgive him anything. Everything. And I would be right back into wondering how he feels about me. Am I only his buddy? Or am I more than that? First he kisses me and then he shoves flowers in my chest. He's constantly back and forth, and I'm in no mood to forgive him. I'm tired of this whole fucking thing. I'm tired of wondering.

Chapter 10

I pull on my swim trunks and grab a towel. My mind won't let go of how I left things with Adam. It just keeps spinning and spinning, every little detail replaying again and again. If I ever needed my midnight swim, it's now.

Knowing that the barbeque ended hours ago, I expect no one to be at the pool.

I step out of my place and instantly see I'm wrong. Someone is at the pool. Adam is sitting on the bench, the same bench where he kissed me.

Damn. Just another reason why I need to swim my laps. Hell, he's the *only* reason if I'm honest with myself. Seeing him reminds me how passionate our kiss was and how much I want to taste his lips again. But that isn't possible. Not after all that has happened between us. I just don't want to see him. Before I get a chance to go back into my apartment, Adam stands and waves at me.

So much for trying to sneak away without being seen.

"Hey, Oliver. I've been waiting for you."

"Why do you keep doing this to me? I just want to swim, Adam. I don't want to talk," I lie, because I really do want to talk to him. *I need to talk to him.* But I'm afraid that talking will only make things worse between us. So I just dive into the pool and start swimming.

After several laps, I look up and see Adam is back on the bench. *Waiting for me.* I realize I can't avoid this any longer —avoid him.

I get out of the water, dry off, and walk to the bench. "I see you're not going to let this go until we talk. Go ahead. Talk. So we can get this over with."

Adam looks at me with his big gorgeous eyes. "You're not going to make this easy, are you?"

"I believe that's all I've been doing, making things easy for you. I told you that I'm done. What else is there to talk about?" I remain standing.

"I deserve this. I don't expect you to forgive me but I hope you will. I'm sorry for how I treated you. It's just that I don't know who I am. I don't understand me. You've been nothing but nice and I've been a total jerk."

"This is the third time you've said that to me. Very true." Now I'm being a bit of a jerk but I can't help myself. I'm still upset.

"I've only known a few gays in the military. They weren't the kind of guys I wanted to be friends with, always cheating on each other. I dated one guy, in secret, of course. I really liked him and I thought our relationship was growing. But when I found him in bed with one of our friends, I felt like an idiot. He actually asked me to join them. That's not who I am, Oliver."

"That sucks, but do you actually think all gay men cheat?"

"I did, I guess. It was the only examples I ever saw. But after meeting you, I now see I was wrong. I've had to play this role for so long, I don't know how to do anything else."

"What are you talking about? What role?"

"The role I had to play because of the military's policy of don't ask, don't tell."

"Bullshit. That doesn't even exist now. Not since 2011. That's just an excuse."

"You may think it is, but that's all I've known my whole life. In fact, I've been playing this role long before I even joined the

Marines. My grandfather was a Marine. My father was a Marine. So can't you understand why I grew up with don't ask, don't tell?"

"No, I don't understand. Not only are you lying to everyone around you but you're lying to yourself."

He sighs. "You're right but there's more to it than just that. The Pentagon may have ended the don't ask, don't tell policy, but it is still in force in my grandfather's mind."

"Your grandfather? What does he have to do with this?"

"After my dad was killed, his father took me and my mother into his home. Her parents were dead. We had absolutely nowhere to go."

Hearing his story breaks my heart, though I'm still upset with him. "I can relate. There was a time, not that long ago, when I had nowhere to go. I know how hard that can be."

"I was only an infant but as I grew up my mother told me many times how wonderful my grandfather was to us back then. I'm very close to my granddad, and he and Mom are, too. Mom still lives with him to this very day."

"I never knew my grandparents. They were dead before I was born. I was an only child, too. Like you." An image of my stone-faced parents standing in their doorway when they kicked me out burns fresh in my mind. I wish I had family who cared about me then. Thank God, I found someone who did care for me, who rescued me. *Malcolm.* I glance at his tree, silently wishing for his presence. If anyone would know how to deal with Adam, it would be Malcolm.

"I lived with Granddad until I graduated from high school and joined the Marines. I've never seen him cry before except the day I shipped out." Adam pauses, obviously reliving that day. "He is a terrific grandfather to me, Oliver. He taught me about fishing, cars, football, and so much more. But he isn't perfect. I can't tell you how many times I've heard my grandfather and his friends tell jokes about gays. My dream was to be a Marine, to honor my father's memory. So I did what I thought I had to do. I buried my feelings so deep I didn't know what I was anymore. Gay or straight? Until I saw you."

Until he saw me? My anger evaporates and I sit down next to him. "I guess we've all gone through difficult times because of who we are."

"Yes, we have, but I don't want you to think I had a terrible childhood. I had a wonderful childhood. I have some great memories. I will always treasure the pride in Granddad's voice when he told me stories about my dad. So can't you understand why I can't ever tell him?"

"It's not that I don't understand, but it still doesn't make it right. It's not your job to make your grandfather comfortable in his bigotry, Adam."

"You're right, but after him losing his only son, his only child, I can't bring myself to break his heart by admitting I am...I am..."

"Say it, Adam."

He grabs my hand. "I'm gay." And then he leans over and kisses me passionately.

I melt into him, tracing his lips with my tongue.

Adam's phone starts ringing.

Damn. Just when we were getting somewhere.

"Sorry," he says, pulling out his phone. "It's Chief Torres. I guess I better take this."

I nod, hoping the call won't take long.

"Yes, sir." Adam frowns. "I will be there in ten minutes." He ends the call and turns to me. "I have to go. I'm sorry."

"What's wrong?"

"There's been an attack on campus."

Chapter 11

I take off my swimsuit and step into the shower. The warm water feels nice on my skin. I close my eyes. Kissing Adam was like no other kiss I've ever experienced before. I always thought a kiss was a kiss. Fun yes. But this was so much more than that.

Even though I don't fully understand what I'm feeling, I really like it. I smile.

Adam opened up to me—really opened up to me. I understand why he has been hiding his truth for so long. I know there's so much more he needs to get through before he can truly be out, but I'm excited how things are going between us. I want to help him.

I *will* help him.

I shampoo my hair, wondering about Adam's call from Chief Torres. *An attack at the university?* I can't believe it. I'm very concerned. The university doesn't ever have any incidents other than a few students getting drunk on the weekends. Hearing that there was an attack on campus seems unreal. Is it still going on?

I finish washing, hoping Adam stays safe and no one gets hurt. After rinsing my body, I step out of the shower, grab a towel, and dry off. Then I slip on a pair of shorts and a T-shirt. Looking at my reflection in the mirror, I see my hair is a complete mess. I don't care. All I really care about is Adam's safety.

I think about sending him a text to find out what is going on but know that isn't a good idea. He's on the job—a job I helped him get. If something happens to him it will be all my fault. Being a campus police officer isn't normally dangerous, but tonight is apparently a different story. The officers are armed, but that even scares me more.

I check my phone. No word from Adam yet, though he promised before he left to send me a text once he has a free moment. What is going on over there? What is Adam dealing with right now? Like a scene in a crime movie, images of gun-toting thugs chasing Adam down a dark alley flood my mind.

"Oh for God's sake, Oliver. You're being ridiculous." It's a university, not the back alleys of Al Capone's Chicago. Damn it. I'm not going to get any sleep if I keep this up. I'm supposed to have breakfast with Martha and Sarah to talk about their wedding plans first thing in the morning. I need rest. Maybe a little wine will help.

I walk to the kitchen and pour myself a glass. I take a sip and move onto the sofa, turning on my television. Something on HGTV or Animal Planet will surely help me relax. But I settle on an old movie that's just starting on one of the local channels. Perfect. That should lull me to sleep.

Fifteen minutes later, I'm yawning as the guy starts teaching the girl some dance steps.

"We interrupt our regular programming to bring you breaking news from our local university," a male announcer says.

An electric shock shoots up and down my spine. I sit up, wide-awake.

An image of Dallas Hall with panicky students appears with the caption *Shots fired at local university. Seven injured. One in critical condition.*

"We interrupt this program to bring you this update about the shooting," the newscaster says. "On scene is our own Claire Sanchez."

The image switches to a female reporter, who is holding a microphone.

"Claire, what can you tells us?"

"John, the campus remains locked down. No one is allowed in or out. University police have two of the gunmen in custody. The third is still on the loose."

I'm frozen in place, anxious for Adam, when one of the campus police officers steps in front of the reporter. I wish the man was Adam, but he's not. Where is Adam? I'm so worried about him.

The officer orders the reporter to move. "You must go back to the parking lot, miss, with the other reporters. Now."

Shots are heard in the background and the officer grabs the woman and pulls her down behind a car. The image goes black.

I jump to my feet. "Oh God."

"Claire?" The newscaster is visibly shaken. "We've lost our feed but will try to get back to her as soon as possible. To recap, there's been a shooting at——"

I click off the TV. I need to get there. Quick. But they won't let me on campus. What can I do? There's absolutely nothing I can do but wait. I feel so helpless.

"Damn it, Adam. Text me. Let me know you're safe." I stare at my phone's screen, willing it to tell me something. But it doesn't ring and no text shows up. Though I probably shouldn't send him a text right now, I can't help myself. I need to know something. Anything. I start to type a message when a knock on my door startles me.

"Thank God," I say, expecting Adam to be on the other side. I bolt to my front door.

When I open it, I don't see Adam.

Instead, a very worried Martha stands in front of me. "Oh, Oliver." She hugs me. "I'm so glad you're home and not at the campus. I knew you would never be there at this hour, but when S and I saw the news, we decided we had to check on our sweet college kids. We have to make sure everyone is safe."

Sarah comes up beside her. "M, the trio is home, thank God."

"We still need to check on Trace and Jackson," Martha says.

"I bet they're home," I tell them.

Martha shakes her head. "I know we are acting like two old mother hens, but we just have to be positive."

I slip on my sandals. "Let's go check on Trace and Jackson together." Until I know if Adam is okay, I'm not going to get any sleep and I definitely don't want to be alone.

Their lights are on. We knock on the door.

Trace opens it. "You were obviously worried about us, but we're fine. I'm glad to see you because we were worried about you, too. We're watching the news. Come on in."

As we walk in the door, Josh, Chad, and Franki come up behind us.

"Room for three more?" Chad asks Trace.

"Definitely. I'll start a pot of coffee."

When we enter the living room, I see that we are not the first to arrive. Eli and Tony are sitting on the couch next to Jackson. All three are glued to the television, which is playing the same movie I was watching earlier.

"Looks like the gang is all here except for Doc and the Marine," Tony says in a concerned tone. "Has anyone heard from them?"

"Jaris is working a double at the hospital." Sarah hands a cup of coffee to Martha.

"And Adam is at the campus." I feel my concern for him multiply. "We were at the pool talking when the chief called him in."

"Has there been any update, guys?" Josh asks. "Have they found the other gunman yet?"

"No updates yet." Jackson moves off the couch to the floor, offering his seat to Martha. "We haven't heard anything new."

"What about the students who were shot?" Martha asks. "Have they given their names yet?"

"Not yet," Eli answered. "But we do know that six out of the seven are stable and only one is in critical condition."

"Quiet, everyone." Martha holds up her hand. "They're breaking in with another update."

The same woman I saw earlier on my TV is standing in a parking lot at the campus I recognize. "We are moments away from hearing from the university's president, Kathleen Anderson, and other officials concerning the shooting, John."

The picture switches to president Anderson standing at a

podium with several microphones. "It's been a horrible tragedy for us this evening. I want to remind our students, faculty, and the public that the campus remains closed until further notice. I'm going to turn this over to the university's Chief of Police, Steve Torres, who is the lead on this operation."

My heart thuds in my chest as I watch as Chief Torres move to the podium. *Please God, let Adam be safe.*

"After I give you the update about this situation, I will be taking your questions," he says. "I'm glad to report that the third and final gunman has been apprehended and is in custody."

Several reporters shout questions at him.

"Thank God," Sarah and Martha say in unison.

"Please hold your questions," the chief tells the reporters. "Officer Adam Stockton apprehended the gunman in Dallas Hall without further incident, where the suspect was holding two students and one professor hostage."

Relief washes over me. Adam is okay. Silently I mouth Sarah and Martha's words, "Thank God."

"Our Marine?" Chad claps his hands. "He's a hero."

"No, Chad. Adam's not *our* Marine." Tony smiles.

I'm a little shocked. The MMA fighter rarely smiles. "What do you mean?"

"He's *your* Marine, Oliver."

"Tony, don't start that again," Chad scolds.

"It's fine," I say and turn back to Tony. "He's not *my* Marine yet, but he is *our* neighbor."

Tony nods. "And a hero."

The chief continues, "Understand that this is still an active crime scene that we are investigating and we ask you to be patient. We will provide additional details as we are able. I can take your questions now."

"Can you tell us the conditions of the hostages Officer Stockton rescued?" one reporter asks.

"They are fine. Just a little shook up, which is understandable. They've been taken to Parkland for observation."

Another reporter stands. "How long will the campus remain

locked down?"

"I can't answer that yet. This is a crime scene. We ask that the public, as well as our students and faculty, give us time to finish our work."

"When do you expect classes to resume?" the editor of the university's newspaper, who I recognize, asks.

"I'm not sure, but classes will be suspended until further notice."

"Do you know the names of the victims?" another reporter asks.

"We do but won't be releasing their names at this time. We want to notify their families first."

"Do you know the other victims' conditions?"

Chief Torres motions for another man to come to the podium. "Let me introduce you to Dr. Gupta, Chief of Surgery at Parkland, to answer those questions."

Dr. Gupta clears his throat. "Besides the three hostages who were admitted moments ago, seven patients are being cared for at Parkland Hospital, five women and three men, ranging in age from eighteen to forty-two. Six of the seven are in stable condition and are expected to have a full recovery. One twenty-six-year-old female remains in critical condition."

Chad shakes his head. It's obvious that we are all having trouble wrapping our heads around this. "Do you think we know any of the victims?"

"Probably," I say, wondering who the seven might be.

Franki puts her arm around Chad. "It's going to be all right."

"Chief, we have heard that the gunmen targeted gays and lesbians at the campus in response to the Supreme Court's ruling yesterday on same-sex marriage. Is this being consider a hate crime?"

My heart sinks. "I didn't know that. I can't believe this happened."

The chief steps back to the microphones. "It's too early to say until we finish our investigation."

I feel my phone vibrate. I look on the screen and see it's from Jaris, Mockingbird Place's resident doctor. "Hello?"

"Oliver, you need to get to the hospital. Candy's been shot."

Chapter 12

Some of the family members of the shooting victims are in the waiting room with me. This horrible night has bonded us together in a strange way. We share in a common tragedy.

The hospital and police have placed the other victims' family members and me here so that we can get updates quickly. According to the doctors, six of the seven are going to make full recoveries. I know every one of the victims. They are members of the Rainbow Coalition.

A mother and father of the youngest victim, Bianca, rush to the nurse on duty behind the desk with a myriad of anxious questions. Bianca is a young lesbian student who always volunteers for the coalition's rallies and fundraisers.

"Your daughter is going to be fine," the nurse reassures them. "She's in recovery right now, but as soon as they take her to her room, you can see her. I'll notify her doctor that you are here. He'll be happy to answer your questions."

I'm glad their daughter is going to be okay. I know that more parents and family will continue to arrive.

I'm the only one here for the seventh victim, Candy, who is the last still in surgery. Her condition remains critical.

Candy's parents died when she was still a teenager. Except for a cousin in Buffalo, New York, she's got no family. I spoke to him a few hours ago. He said he was sorry to hear about her situation, but he just couldn't make it at this time. Having no real family is probably the reason Candy bonded with me so quickly. She really is my big sister. Nothing or no one will ever change that.

The new arrivals take a seat, arm in arm, comforting each other about their Bianca's condition.

The phone on the nurse's desk rings. The crowd turns her direction, hanging on every word she speaks.

"Family of Candy Fleming?"

"I'm here." I step to the desk, my heart pounding in my chest.

"They have an update for you." She hands me the receiver.

"I'm here for Candy Fleming."

"Oliver, this is Jaris."

"Oh God, Jaris. What's happening?"

"Dr. Patterson is doing all he can for her, but it doesn't look good. Do you know if she would want a priest or pastor to be here?"

"Priest? Oh my God, Jaris." A sudden wave of weakness and nausea moves through me. I grip the edge of the desk, willing myself not to pass out. "She's not going to make it?"

"We don't know yet. We can't seem to stop the internal bleeding. We've given her transfusions, but she is losing more blood than we can give her."

"God, this can't be happening." I swallow hard, knowing I'm about to lose it. "I believe she'd want a priest since she was raised Catholic, even though she's been out of the church for years. You can understand why."

"I do understand. I'm going to call my priest. Father Michaels is also understanding about us. I'll call back if anything changes."

"Call *my* phone, please. I just need a moment."

"I understand, Oliver."

I grip the receiver as the line goes dead. I'm frozen in place. I can't move. I feel paralyzed, though I need to get out of the waiting room. I need to find a place to go before I fall apart in front of these people. I'm on the brink of crying my eyes out. I don't want to do that here. *I can't do that here.* Candy wouldn't want me to make a scene. She's tough. God, I just lost Malcolm. I don't want to lose her.

"Are you all right, young man?" the nurse asks me.

I can't speak. Can't move. Can't breathe.

And then I feel a hand on my shoulder.

"Oliver, you're white as a sheet." Standing before me in his uniform, Adam takes the phone from me and hands it to the nurse. He wraps his arms around me. "I'm getting you out of here."

I nod. *Adam is here.*

He leads me out of the waiting room. Once we are in the hallway, I can't hold back my agony any longer and begin sobbing in his arms.

Adam pulls me in tighter. "It's going to be okay. I know it is."

"I hope you're right, but it doesn't look good for Candy." I tell him what Jaris said and look in his eyes. "I was so worried about you. You could have been shot."

"But I wasn't," he says.

"Thank God. I'm in awe of you, Adam Stockton. You saved those men in Afghanistan and now you saved those hostages from that gunman. You're a true-blue hero."

"Hardly. Just doing my job. That's all. Your color is coming back. Do you feel better now?"

"Some."

He points to the empty chairs at the end of the hallway and puts his arm around my shoulder. "Let's go sit there. We can have some privacy and talk."

As we walk to the chairs I say, "I'm so glad you came."

"I wouldn't be anywhere else. You should know that."

I nod and we sit side by side quietly for a few moments.

"Can I get you something?" Adam asks. "Coffee? Soda? Something to eat?"

"No thanks. I don't need anything now that you're here."

He grabs my hand. "I'm here. Here for you. Whatever you need."

"I need to try to understand why this happened. Adam, I know all the victims. They are members of the Rainbow Coalition. It's obvious this is a hate crime."

"Yes, although the department isn't stating that yet. The three gunmen are part of a radical online religious group on the FBI's watch list. They call themselves the Knights of the True Faith. It's sickening." Adam brings out his phone. "This is their blog. Total trash."

I stare at the emblem on the screen, a black swastika on top of a crucifix, and feel my old pain resurface.

Adam shakes his head. "These jerks claim to be the only true believers in America. They hate everyone—gays and lesbians, blacks and Hispanics, Jews and Muslims. You name the group, you'll see it on their hit list. I just find it hard to believe that people can have so much hate."

"They can. I've seen it firsthand." I gaze into his eyes. "My own parents were filled with the same kind of bigotry." I bring out my billfold, pulling out the yellowed paper with my poem and hand it to him. "I was thirteen when I wrote this, living on a boys ranch my parents sent me to. I've kept it to remind me how far I've come and to never hold onto bitterness."

Adam silently reads the short piece that I memorized long ago.

TRAPPED INSIDE.
My heartbeat is falling behind,
As the life that surrounds me
Morphs into the insanity
I so desperately try to leave behind
In my dreams.

OVERCOME by stimulation
The senses retreat,
Not accepting the reality
I made out to be make-believe.
Sorrows no longer comforted

By failed attempts
To erase your mistakes.

YOU HAVE NO CHOICE,
As your voice is replaced
By the glares that have
Followed you from the past.

ADAM LOOKS at me with sad eyes and slowly hands the poem back to me. "You wrote this when you were only thirteen?"

I nod, folding the paper neatly and placing it back in my wallet.

"It's excellent, but I can't imagine what hell you must have been going through to be able to write a dark poem like this at such a young age."

"My father was, and still is, as far as I know, a deacon in the Baptist church back home. He and my mother are leaders in that church and in the community. I came out to them when I was thirteen. You should have seen the look of rage on their faces. From that day on, they saw me as a sinner who needed to be rescued from hell. The very next day they shipped me off to one of those organizations that promises to make gays turn straight. You wouldn't believe the hell I had to go through."

I WIPE my eyes on my pillowcase. They are swollen from crying. I look at the bruises on my arms, legs and the rest of my body that my father gave me when I told him and my mother the truth. "I'm gay."

He just kept beating me, quoting bible verses and screaming for the demons to come out of me while my mother watched without saying a word to stop him.

I feel so alone. Afraid.

I wish I hadn't told them. They don't understand. I can't change who I am. I'm gay. I've known it for some time. And they won't change who they are either. Bigots. They see me as an abomination. What am I going to do? I can't stay here. I've been saving all my money from mowing lawns to buy a computer some day. I have three hundred twenty-six dollars and seventy-seven cents. I've hidden it in a coffee can underneath our house in the crawl space. That's probably enough money for a bus ticket out of Winters. Even if it is, where can I go? How can I make it on my own? I'm only thirteen.

I hear my parents in the other room—their voices are loud and full of anger and disappointment. They've been awake all night. They called our pastor. Why? Do they think he has some special power or prayer that will miraculously change me? They're wrong. It's not possible. How many times did I beg God to make me different, to take away the feelings I was having? Hundreds, maybe thousands. But I never changed and the feelings stayed. God made me this way. I'm not a mistake. I don't want to change, even if I could.

I hear a loud knocking at our front door and look at my radio clock on my nightstand. It's four-thirty in the morning. Who could it be? Pastor Westburg?

My bedroom door flies open and two big men in cowboy hats charge into my room. I don't know them. They are strangers.

I'm so scared.

"Get dressed!" the taller of the two shouts at me.

My parents are standing in the hall behind the two men.

"Mom! Dad! What's going on?"

They don't answer.

The tall man glares at me. "Did you hear me, Oliver? Get dressed. Now."

"Why?"

The other man pulls me off my bed and I fall to the floor. He looks down at me. "We ask the questions, not you. Move. We're not going to say it again."

I glance at my parents, wishing they would save me. But they won't. These men are here to take me away because of them. Who are they? Where are they going to take me?

Terrified, I curl my fist and begin pounding on the one closest to me as hard as I can.

He grabs me by the wrists. "So this is how you're going to play this out. I would have preferred the easy way, Oliver, but you're making that impossible. This is for your own good, son."

Tears stream down my cheeks. "Please. Don't do this to me."

"Do you need his suitcase?" my mother asks them, and all hope for rescue from this nightmare disappears.

"No, ma'am. He'll be wearing new clothes at the ranch."

"Ranch? What ranch?"

"I told you not to ask questions." The man holding me by the wrists squeezes tight, causing me pain. I know two more bruises will be added to the others my father already gave me.

I realize there's nothing I can do to change this situation. Until I can, I decide to give in to their demands. "I'll get dressed."

Five minutes later, they stuff me into the back of a white van and speed away from the only home I've ever known. I stare out the back window at my parents and wonder why they let this happen to me. Do they hate me that much?

My kidnappers have made it very clear that I'm not supposed to ask questions, but I don't care. This is already hell. "Where are you taking me?"

"A place to save you from the devil's claws and eternal damnation, boy," the tall one answers.

They drive the van onto a dirt road ninety minutes later. Another fifteen, they pull up in front of a large building that looks like a barn to me. There's nothing else in sight. We are out in the middle of West Texas. Even if I could run away to the next town, I wouldn't know what direction to head in.

My captors force me out of their white van.

"Welcome to your future, boy," the tall one says with a big smile on his ugly face. "Those impure thoughts you've been having will be a thing of the past. You'll see. Trust us."

I don't trust them. Not one bit.

The one who grabbed my wrists puts his arm around my shoulders like we're friends all of a sudden. "The Water of Truth Ranch is going to make a God-fearing man out of you no matter how long it takes."

"OH MY GOD, OLIVER. HOW HORRIBLE." Adam puts his arms around me. "How long were you there?"

"Twenty-four months and fifteen days." I sigh. "I liked some of it. The horses. Riding. Some of the other boys. But most of it was pretty awful. For the first several weeks I ended up in what the ranchers called 'Joshua's Well,' a windowless shack away from the bunkhouse and barn. We boys called it 'solitary' or the 'hole.'"

"Why did they put you there?"

"For talking to other boys. We weren't allowed to speak to each other until the ranchers gave us permission, and that didn't happen until they thought they'd cured us from homosexuality."

"Fucking assholes."

"You can say that again."

"Did your parents ever come to visit you?"

"No. They wrote letters that were filled with passages from the bible and told me how they were praying for me. After a year and a half, I realized I wasn't ever going to be free without pretending that living on the ranch had changed me and made me straight. So I did. I faked it. It took me six months to convince them, but it worked."

"You went home?"

"Yes. For one day and one night. I got the money out of the coffee can I'd hidden under the house. The next day I hitchhiked out of Winters and caught a bus in Abilene for Dallas."

"You were only fifteen. God, I can't imagine how hard that was on you. What happened when you got to Dallas?"

My gut tightens. I can't tell him that.

"Oliver, are you okay? The color drained out of your face again."

"I'm fine. It's just hard thinking about the past. I survived and eventually met Malcolm. The rest is history."

My phone rings. It's Jaris.

"Great news, Oliver," he says. "We stopped the bleeding. Candy is going to make it."

"Really?"

"Yes, really. She's stable now."

I'm elated. "When can I see her?"

"Not until tomorrow. You should go home and get some rest. I'll text you when you can see her."

"Thanks, Jaris." I turn to Adam. "She's going to be fine."

He hugs me. "Thank God."

His phone buzzes.

"It's the chief," he tells me and answers the call. "Hello, sir."

I look in his eyes and realize how crazy I am about him. I wouldn't have made it through the last hour without him being by my side.

"I'm at the hospital with Oliver right now. I will, Chief." Adam turns to me. "He wants me to put the phone on speaker so he can talk to you and me both."

"Hi, Chief."

"Oliver, how is Candy doing?"

"I just got word she's going to be okay."

"Thank God. Do you need anything, son?"

"I'm fine. I'm just glad no one got killed."

"You and me both. Adam, I need you back at the station as soon as possible. The FBI just officially deemed the shooting a hate crime."

"Good," Adam I and say in unison.

"I agree. The feds read your initial report but they still need to interview you."

"Do you need a ride back home?" Adam asks me.

"No. I have my car. Go. I'll be all right."

"Promise to go home and get some sleep."

I nod, glad that he cares.

"Chief, I'll be there in twenty minutes."

Adam walks with me to my car.

I open the door. "You can't imagine how much it means to me that you came."

He leans in and kisses me tenderly. "Where else would I be?"

Chapter 13

C andy has been sleeping soundly since the nurses brought her into the room from Recovery. Her prognosis is so good. Her hospital room is filled with flowers and balloons wishing her a speedy recovery. Holding her hand, I sit in a chair next to her bed. Martha and Sarah are sitting in the other two chairs.

"I'm thinking pink roses for our bouquets," Sarah says. "What do you think about that, Oliver?"

Since we know how well Candy is doing, we are extremely relaxed. All the previous tension is gone. So to pass the time until Candy awakens, we are planning Martha and Sarah's wedding.

"Sounds beautiful," I say. "How many guests are you going to invite?"

Martha smiles and grabs Sarah's hand. "We want an intimate ceremony—just the regular gang. I want Red Shimmer to play at the party and I would love to ask Adam if he would sing a song."

In my mind I can hear his smooth baritone voice singing those K-5 hits again, and it makes me happy.

"M, that's a great idea. Adam can sing like an angel." Sarah looks at me. "Do you think he'll agree to sing at the party?"

"Party?" Candy's eyes open. "What party? And what am I supposed to bring?"

I'm thrilled she's awake. "Nothing. We're just talking about Martha and Sarah's wedding next Sunday." I look into her eyes and say a silent prayer of thanks. "And the doctors think you should be up and about by then."

"Thank God. I wouldn't miss their wedding for anything, even if I had to be rolled in on a gurney."

"I'm glad to see your sassiness is still intact," I say, squeezing her hand.

"You didn't think a couple of bullets would get me down." She grins and then a look of seriousness appears on her face. "Is everyone else okay?"

"Yes, sweetheart." Martha nods. "Everyone has been released except for you and Bianca. But she should be going home tomorrow. You, on the other hand, have a few more days in here."

"Why? I feel fine." Candy tries to sit up and groans.

"Hold your horses, sis." I leave the chair and brush the hair out of her eyes. "You're tough but you still need to take things slow for now." I help her use the controls on the bed to raise her head. "That better?"

"Much. Thanks. Oliver, did they capture the shooters?"

"Yes. All three of them. Adam got the last one and rescued three people," I tell her with pride.

"I'm not surprised. He's a Marine. Where is he?"

"Home asleep," I say. "He was up all night with the FBI, but we still sent each other some texts. He wanted to come with me this morning to see you, but I knew he needed rest. He's going to be very busy the next several days according to the chief."

"The FBI is involved?"

"They are and have deemed the shooting a hate crime."

"Oh God. I'm the one who got everyone together." Tears well up in her eyes. "I'm to blame for this."

Sarah leans over the bed. "Don't say that, Candy. The only ones to blame for this are behind bars. You didn't do anything wrong. You were just trying to organize a celebration."

Her doctor enters the room. "How's my patient doing today?"

"I'm fine. Thanks."

He steps close. "Then why the tears? Are you in pain?"

"No. I'm just a little overwhelmed."

"I'm Dr. Patterson." He points to the device attached to her I.V. "If you have pain, you can push this button to get a dose of morphine. It won't release more than you need, so you can't overdose."

"Thanks, Doctor. I've seen these before."

He takes her vitals. "You're quite a remarkable woman, Candy. I'm glad to see you're doing so well. There's someone who wants to speak with you about your heroic act. Are you up to talking with him for a few minutes?"

"Yes, but I'm no hero."

Dr. Patterson grins. "Humble. Of course you are. I heard what happened. If you hadn't jumped between the shooter and that young girl, she wouldn't have made it. You *are* a hero, Candy."

"This is the first I'm hearing about this." I'm stunned.

Candy shrugs. "Bianca and I were hanging rainbow flags at the Student Union when the shooters started firing. I did what I had to do."

"*Semper fi.*" I think about Adam. I never dreamed I would know a hero, let alone two heroes.

"I'll be right back with your special guest." Dr. Patterson walks to the door. "Are you sure you're up for this?"

"I feel quite well under the circumstances."

"Very good," he says and leaves.

"I wonder who this special guest could be," Candy asks. "Do you know, Oliver?"

"No, I haven't a clue, but I bet it's a reporter. You are a hero after all."

"It's not being a hero doing your job," she says. "Once a Marine always a Marine."

"So I've been told." I think about Adam.

Candy looks at me. "Oliver, what day is this?"

"Sunday," I tell her. "You only lost a day."

"What time?"

"Eleven in the morning."

"The parade starts at three. I should be there." She sighs. "Or are we still having a parade?"

"Sweetie, it's all taken care of." I squeeze her hand. "Yes, the parade is on. Everyone has pulled together. Melody and Ashley took over and you can't imagine how much love and support we're receiving from the university as well as the community."

"Do you think having a parade after what happened is a good idea?"

"It's a great idea," Sarah says. "It's a must idea. We can't let the haters shove us back into the shadows."

"Don't worry, Candy," Martha adds. "The campus police as well as the city police have volunteered to escort us and secure the parade route. The mayor and all the city council members are coming too."

"Are you serious?"

"Yes," I tell her. "And all the local stations are covering the event. So, you'll be able to watch the parade from your bed." My phone buzzes. "It's Melody. Hello?"

"Oliver, you're not going to believe this," Melody states in a loud, excited voice.

"Not going to believe what?"

"The vice president is in Dallas. He came for a fundraiser this morning and he's staying this afternoon so he can attend Candy's parade."

"You can't be serious?"

"What's wrong?" Candy asks.

A knock on the door stops me from answering.

Martha opens it and finds three men in suits.

"Ma'am, I'm Agent Collins. We're from the Secret Service. We need to secure the room."

I nod and smile. "He's here, Melody."

"Who's there?" Melody asks.

"You-know-who," I answer, not wanting to ruin the surprise for Candy.

"Really?"

"Yes, really."

"What's going on?" Candy asks.

"Dr. Patterson wasn't kidding." I grab her hand. "You're about to meet someone very special."

Once the Secret Service men are satisfied the room is safe and the camera crew comes in, the vice president and Dr. Patterson enter.

The look of shock on Candy's face is priceless. I hope the cameraman filmed it.

"So this is our hero." The vice president smiles. "It's my honor and pleasure to meet you, Ms. Fleming."

"Please, call me Candy, your honor. I mean sir. Mr. Vice President."

"Only if you'll call me 'Joe.'"

She shakes her head. "Oh, I couldn't do that. I just couldn't."

I chuckle quietly. I've never seen her so excited and flustered before.

"I just spoke to the president. He wants me to convey how proud he is of you."

"The president of the United States is proud of me? He knows my name."

The vice president grins. "Yes, he does. In fact, the entire country knows your name, Candy. And the president and First Lady would like to invite you and Officer Stockton and the other officers who acted with such courage and valor to the White House after your recovery. He wants to show his appreciation and to honor you for your heroism."

I'm so happy that she and Adam and the other officers will be recognized at such a high level for what they did. They deserve it.

"Thank you, sir," Candy says. "It would be my pleasure, but I'm really not a hero. Just doing my job."

"And what a magnificent job you did. I understand that you are vice president of the Rainbow Student Coalition at the university."

"I am. And this is the president," she says, pointing at me. "My

113

best friend, Oliver. And two of our dearest friends, Martha and Sarah."

The vice president shakes our hands and asks us questions.

When he learns that Martha and Sarah are getting married next Sunday, he says, "Congratulations. I'm so glad that you are able to celebrate your love of each other more fully in this state thanks to the Supreme Court's ruling, but there is clearly more work that needs to be done. The tragedy at the campus proves that." He looks at me. "And Mr. President, thank you for your good work, in particular with Lifeline. It's young people like you and organizations like yours that will make the difference."

His words overwhelm me. "Thank you, sir."

Agent Collins leans forward and says to him, "Mr. Vice President, we need to be going."

"Of course. When I came to Dallas, I had no idea I would be in the company of such wonderful people. It has certainly been my pleasure meeting you." He turns to Candy. "Especially meeting you, Candy. Get well soon. I look forward to seeing you again in Washington."

I SHAKE hands with all the parade volunteers and thank them for their hard work. Because of the vice president's attendance, the parade was a huge success and got national coverage on all the major networks and cable news channels. The exposure is going to be great for the coalition and for Lifeline.

"How's Candy doing?" Ashley asks me.

"Fantastic," I answer. "Her doctor thinks she might even get released by Thursday."

"That's such good news." Melody finishes putting away the last of the rainbow flags in the boxes. "From all the calls I've received, I understand that you can't turn on a television without seeing footage with Candy and the vice president."

"I got to catch a little of it in the Student Union right before the parade started," Ashley says. "Candy has no idea how much she's helped the LGBTQIA community because of her heroism."

"We're all so proud of her." It's good to hear Ashley use all the abbreviations without hesitation. She and Melody have made a complete turnaround on that issue. "Candy's shown the world that we are just like anyone else."

Melody nods. "I have no doubt that there are big things waiting for her after she recovers."

"What else needs to be cleaned up?" I ask them.

"We've got the rest of it." Ashley puts her hand on my shoulder. "You need to get back to the hospital and check on our girl."

"Are you sure?"

"Absolutely. I bet Candy's anxious to talk to you about the parade."

Melody grins. "I have no doubt after watching it on television she's got ideas about next year's parade."

"Next year's?" I ask.

"Yep," she answers. "We took a straw vote and everyone wants to make this an annual event. And best of all, we want to name it Candy Fleming's University Pride Parade."

I laugh. "She's going to have a hundred reasons why we should call it something else, you know."

"We know," they say in unison.

"But that's the name," Melody states firmly.

"I'm glad. I'll call you when I get to the hospital and let you know how she's doing."

Walking to my car, I send an emoticon of a smiley face to Adam. I haven't seen him since last night at the hospital. He's been so busy with the FBI's investigation and with all the interviews he's had to give.

A text pops up on my screen from him. *Miss you.*

Reading those two words gives me the tingles. *When can I see you?*

Very busy. Call you later. Then the next thing that appears on my phone is a red heart from him.

A sudden flash of warmth spreads through my body. I'm so

wrapped up in what I'm feeling, I spread my arms wide and spin around in the parking lot next to my car. Realizing what a silly thing I just did, I look around. Thank God, no one saw me, but it doesn't change the fact that I'm happy. Very happy. I can't wait for Adam to call me.

Chapter 14

I walk into Candy's hospital room. I'm shocked and pleased to see her sitting in one of the chairs drinking from a coffee cup. Franki, who is on the schedule that Martha and I set up to stay with our special patient, is sitting in one of the other chairs. We want to make certain Candy is never alone.

"Look," Franki says. "It's the Parade Master."

"Parade Master?" I'm confused.

Candy smiles. "Do you realize you're still wearing a rainbow lei, Oliver?"

I glance down and take it off. "We did want publicity." I put it around her neck. "What did you think of the parade?"

"It looked great. I'm so proud of everyone." She takes a sip from her cup.

"I leave you for a few hours and this is what I find—you sitting in a chair drinking coffee. What kind of patient are you?"

"Dr. Patterson's orders," she says. "He also told me to get up and walk around. The nurses and I walked around the hallway. I want to do one more lap before I get back in that miserable bed. Want to come with me and Franki?"

"Sis, have you forgotten that you were shot? You don't need to push yourself so hard."

"I *was* shot, Oliver. But that's in the past. My job now is to get well and back on my feet."

Franki stands. "Oliver, if you're going to stick around for a bit I'll go grab a bite to eat from the cafeteria and give you and Candy some alone time."

"Thanks. I'd like that."

Franki hugs Candy gently and then pats me on the back.

After she leaves, Candy looks up at me. "We have so many exciting things to do—Martha and Sarah's wedding, the trip to Washington to meet the president and First Lady, and we still have the fall semester ahead of us with a charter to change."

"You're wearing me out just mentioning all those things. We just had the parade, Candy. Can't we just breathe for—"

"Yes, while we're walking down the hall together."

I shake my head. "I guess I'm not going to win this battle."

"You got that right, Mr. President. Help me get my I.V. pole."

She takes my hand and we walk out into the hallway. "Have you seen Adam yet?"

"Not yet, but we did text each other. Candy, he said he missed me and sent a red heart."

"That's wonderful news. I'm so happy for you. He's a great guy."

"Yes he is." I'm impressed how tough she is but not surprised. "How far do you want to go?"

"All the way to Washington, DC." She laughs. "Oh, that hurts. Laughing hurts."

"Then don't laugh." I hold on to her tight.

She keeps smiling. "But I want to laugh. You know it's the best medicine."

"You're too much. I wasn't asking about upcoming trips. I want to know how far in this hallway you want to go."

"Just around the nurses' station. That's about all I can muster right now. But about DC, I want you to go with me and Adam."

"I can't go with you, Sis. First of all, I wasn't invited. And second of all, I do not want to take away from you, Adam, and the others by being there. I'm no hero."

"No hero? The hell you're not. I can think of several things you've done that make you a hero, Oliver. For one, you set up Lifeline. Just think of all the homeless teens we've gotten off the streets."

"I only got the ball rolling with Malcolm's help. I'm not even on the board anymore."

"Maybe not, but it was your idea and you still volunteer. Besides, you've even put yourself in danger more times than I can count going to the worse sections of Dallas to rescue these kids. Hell, you just saved that teenager from El Paso last month. You remember."

"Tommy. Poor kid is only fourteen. He was in bad shape. So skinny."

"Right. Tommy. His family kicked him out just because he tells them he's gay? I still don't understand how parents can be so cruel to their own children."

"I can't either," I say, thinking about my own parents rejecting me.

"Tommy was living under a bridge and hadn't eaten in days. Those three thugs were beating him up and you ran right in without thinking about your own safety, with just pepper spray and your fists, and rescued him. That might not have made the news like mine did but that doesn't make you any less of a hero."

"Like you said to me, sis. I was just doing my job."

"You've got the heart of a Marine, Oliver. I've known that since I met you." She smiles at me. "Think of all the good we can accomplish if we go to DC together. The coalition, Lifeline, and university will get national attention. Just because we won the marriage equality fight doesn't mean our battles are over. That's what the Vice President said to us."

"I remember. Let me think about it."

"At least you're not saying 'no.'" She winks. "I have an idea who will get you over to my way of thinking."

"Oh you do, do you?" I can tell she's getting tired when we walk back into her room.

"Yes, I do. Our favorite Marine will be able to convince you."

"That's not playing fair. You know how I feel about Adam."

"When did you ever know me to play fair?"

"Never. Seems like I'm losing every battle today with you, but there's one I will not lose. That's getting you back into that *miserable* bed."

"I'm not going to fight you on that. I'm very tired."

After I fluff her pillows and pull the covers up for her, my phone buzzes.

"It's a text from Adam," I say, unable to keep the excitement out of my voice. I look down and see that's she's already asleep just as Franki walks back in the room.

"Oh good," Franki says in hushed tone. "She needs her sleep."

"Yes, she does. Do you need anything before I take off?"

"No. I'm good."

"Call me if you think of something."

"I will. Martha and Sarah are relieving me at midnight."

"Thanks so much for doing this."

"I care a lot about Candy. There's no other place I would be."

I know Franki and Candy are friends, but the look in Franki's eyes makes me wonder if she wants something more.

I step out and close the door. I look at the text from Adam.

Hey. I hate to ask but I need a favor.

I text back, *Absolutely. What?*

Let me call you. Too long to text.

I answer my phone on the first ring. "Hi."

"I hate to ask but I need your help."

"Of course. Anything."

"Oliver, my mom is almost to Dallas." Adam sounds tired. "I'm still stuck at the station with another FBI agent. I can't get ahold of Martha or Sarah. Would you mind meeting my mom and seeing if you can get the key to let her into my place?"

"I'll take care of it, Adam." I remember how he was there for me at the hospital when I needed him most. Now I get a chance to be there for him. "Don't worry about a thing. You're mom's in good hands."

Chapter 15

Driving into Mockingbird Place's parking lot, I pull my car into my spot. When I come around the building, I see a woman sitting on the bench by the pool. She has a suitcase and I recognize her from Adam's photos. She's his mother. The family resemblance is unmistakable. She's got his same dark hair color and smile.

"Hello, Mrs. Stockton. I'm Adam's friend." I fire off a text to Adam to let him know I'm with her.

"Ah. Oliver. Adam sent me a text to expect you." She stands and shakes my hand. "Do you have a key to his place?"

"No. But I know where we can get one—from Martha and Sarah. They're the managers of Mockingbird Place. I hope they're home. If not, you can wait at my apartment until they or Adam return."

"That's very sweet of you to offer. Thank you."

"That's their apartment." I point at their door. "Wait here. I'll be right back."

She nods and sits back down.

I ring the doorbell just as I get a text from Adam.

Thanks, Oliver. I'll call you when I'm through here. I hope it won't be long.

I fire back, *No worries. I'll keep your mom company until you get back.*

The next thing I see on my screen is another red heart.

God, I can't wait to see him. I send a heart back.

A yawning Martha opens the door. "Hi Oliver." A look of worry comes over her. "Is something wrong with Candy?"

"She's fine. Better than fine. I just came over to get Adam's key. His mom has showed up and he's stuck at the station." I motion to Mrs. Stockton, who waves back at us. "He's been trying to call you and Sarah."

"Oh my goodness. We were exhausted after everything and went straight to bed so that we would be ready for the midnight shift at the hospital. I guess we didn't hear our phones ring. Let me get the key for you."

I glance back at Adam's mom. She came early once she heard about the shooting. It's very clear how much she cares about him. I'm glad that he has her in his life.

Martha returns and hands me Adam's key. "Here you go."

"Sorry for waking you." I lean over and kiss her on the cheek. "Now, go back to bed. Get some sleep."

She smiles. "I will. Bye."

I head back to the bench where Adam's mom is waiting. "We're all set, Mrs. Stockton."

I grab her luggage and lead her to his door.

When we walk in, she says, "My goodness, this place looks amazing. Adam told me you decorated it for him." She takes a seat on the sofa, looking in every direction. "Wow. You have an incredible eye."

"It was my pleasure. Even though we've only known each other a short time, Adam has become a good friend to me."

"I'm so glad Adam has found a good friend already."

"Actually, he's found many friends here at Mockingbird Place. We're all very close—sort of like family. No one's family lives in state, so we claim each other." My biological parents live in Texas, but I don't need to tell her that. We just met after all.

"That's nice to hear, but I'm certain you are his *closest* friend. At least that's how it seems to me from the phone conversations I've had with him since he moved in." She leans forward slightly. "That's right, isn't it?"

How do I answer her? She seems to know more than I realize. Did Adam tell her about us? The truth? I don't think so. Not yet. I know firsthand what it takes for a closeted guy to come out. Adam only has one toe out right now. We shared a few kisses—which were great—but there's more work he's got to do before he announces to the world and his mom that he is gay. And his grandfather. A lot more work.

So I decide to be vague when I answer her. "We did hit it off right away and became very good friends."

She grins. "I'll settle with that answer for now."

I like her. She's very genuine. But telling her more—no matter what she suspects or knows—about Adam and my relationship isn't my place. It's Adam's. She's his mother, not mine.

What is our relationship? It's just beginning. We've only shared a few kisses, but I want more, many more.

"Oliver, are you in there?" she asks with a smile, pulling me back from my thoughts. "You seem preoccupied."

"It's been quite a crazy weekend. I'm sorry. Would you like something to drink, Mrs. Stockton?"

"Yes. I wonder if Adam has some wine."

"I know he has beer."

"That's my son. Just like his father."

Hearing her talk about Adam's father reminds me what Adam said about her. Even after such a horrible tragedy losing her husband, she picked up the pieces and made a life for her and her infant son. Adam was right. She is strong and amazing.

"Let me check to see if he has a bottle. If he doesn't have one, I have some wine at my house." I step into the kitchen and find a very nice bottle of wine on the counter. "We're in luck." I pick up the bottle and read the label. "I hope you like Cabernet. This is from the Chappellet winery in Napa."

"Oh my sweet son. He knows me, Oliver. That's my favorite wine."

"I can't wait to try it." I open the drawer where I'd put the opener.

I get two glasses out of the cabinet and fill them with the rich, dark-red liquid. When I return to the living room, I hand Adam's mom one of the glasses, place the open bottle on the coffee table, and sit down beside her on the sofa.

"A toast," she says. "To new friends and new places."

We clink our glasses together and then sip the wine.

I like the taste of it. "This has a very nice flavor, Mrs. Stockton. I'll be buying this for myself."

"I'm so glad you like it. Do you enjoy wine?"

"Very much." I take another sip. "May I offer a toast as well?"

"Of course."

"To your son. The hero."

She smiles broadly. "Here. Here."

After another few sips of the delicious wine, I lean back and smile. I find it very easy to talk to her. "We're all so proud of what your son did at the campus."

"So am I. I understand you helped him get the job at the station."

"I did. He wasn't sure they would want him because of his missing leg. I knew they would, especially with his military background."

"Adam told you about his leg?" She looks surprised.

"Actually, I saw his prosthetics by accident. We had a bit of an argument about that but we've worked it all out. What he did in Afghanistan…it's…amazing. He saved those men."

"I'm glad he told you about that, Oliver. It's something he doesn't share with very many people."

"Yeah. He's very private about that, though I think it would be good if he shared it more."

"I agree, but his grandfather and I haven't been able to get him to open up. He's been closed off since he lost his leg. I've been so worried about him but haven't known what else to do. I was excited when he told me he'd enrolled at the university in Dallas. But then I realized he was just trying to put distance between us. He's never said it but I know he feels broken without his leg."

"Yeah, he told me how hard it's been to deal with. But look what he just did. He's more of a man than most. He saved those people the last shooter was holding hostage."

"Have you seen him on TV?"

"No. I really haven't had a chance, but I know he was great."

She smiles. "He was great. Every interview I saw he seemed so at ease, like he'd been on television his entire life. It's a good thing I didn't find out what was going on until it was all over. I would have been a total basket case of worry."

"I *was* a total basket case of worry. He got the call from the station about the shooting when we were talking on the same bench you were sitting on when I found you. Adam rushed to the campus, and I didn't know what was happening at first. Later, I saw the reports on television about the three gunmen. I tried to reach him but he wasn't answering his cell or responding to my texts."

"Oh my goodness, Oliver. I can only imagine how tough that was on you."

"It was tough. God, I'm so glad that he was safe and no one was killed." I take another sip of my wine.

"I remember when one of his buddies called me and told me about the attack in Afghanistan." She becomes so very quiet. "The doctors had to take his leg and weren't sure if he would make it through the night. There was no way I could get to him. I felt so helpless. I couldn't do anything but pray. I can't explain to you the fear I felt just waiting for the phone to ring and to learn if Adam had survived. It was many hours before someone finally called me to tell me that he made it through the surgery fine." She takes another sip of wine and then refills her glass and mine. "Sorry I got so melancholy. We just met and I'm baring my soul to you. You're very easy to talk to."

"So are you, and I guess we're both good listeners, Mrs. Stockton."

"Please call me, Kathy, short for Katherine."

I clink our glasses together. "To you, Kathy."

"And to you, Oliver."

We take another drink.

I feel warm and relaxed. "Adam is so lucky to have you as his mother."

"And I'm lucky to have him as my son. He is so brave. I couldn't ask for a better son. So much like his dad. He can be stubborn and does have a temper."

"I've experienced a little of that."

"Oh really?"

"I'm sorry. I shouldn't have said that. I guess the wine is loosening my tongue."

She grins. "Mine too. God, I haven't talked about this to anyone but his grandfather."

"Adam has told me a little about your father-in-law." His grandfather was part of the reason Adam felt like he had to remain in the closet.

"He's a very good man."

I'm not so sure about that, but I keep it to myself.

"The military sent Adam to Germany after his surgery. Pop and I flew there to be with him during his recovery and therapy. The physical pain was tough on Adam, but the emotional pain was even harder. He made us promise never to mention that he'd lost his leg to anyone."

"He made me promise the same thing."

Kathy pours the rest of the wine into our glasses.

"I can't believe we drank the whole bottle."

She giggles. "Good listeners and good wine drinkers."

I laugh and take a drink.

"You know you're very handsome and so very nice. Just the kind of guy I want for my son."

I choke on the Cabernet. "What?"

"You are gay, aren't you?"

"Um…yes." I place my empty glass on the coffee table. "I'm just a bit confused."

She laughs, downs the rest of her wine, and sets her empty glass next to mine. "My son doesn't think I know he's gay. But I know. I've known for years. And you're just perfect for him, Oliver."

"You think so?" How in the hell does she know all this?

"Yes." She sighs. "I just wish I could get Adam to trust me enough to tell me. I love my son and it doesn't matter to me that he's gay. I just want him to be happy."

"Why haven't you asked him yourself?"

"I don't know. I suppose it's because I never thought it was any of my business until he was ready to share it with me. I thought he would have told me by now. We've always been so close." She closes her eyes and clasps her hands together. "But he hasn't, and I don't know why."

"I think the reason doesn't matter, Kathy. You both have been dancing around this issue for some time. I can't even dream of how hard it was for you to lose your husband and to become a single parent. But you've done a great job. Adam loves you very much. It's time for all his and your cards to be on the table. Tell him you know. Be direct. That's my advice."

"Do you really think I should?"

"Absolutely, because it doesn't really matter to you. Once it's out in the open, Adam will be able to share with you everything about his life, his truth."

"I think you're right. As soon as the perfect time comes, I'm going to tell him I know."

"Maybe that time will be tonight, Kathy."

Chapter 16

I walk into the kitchen with Adam's mom. I still can't believe how great she is. We've really hit it off. And I loved hearing all the stories about Adam when he was a little boy.

"Kathy, you really don't have to cook for me."

"But I want to make dinner for you and Adam. Besides, I love to cook," she says.

"So do I."

"Why am I not surprised? We are a lot a like, you and I." She smiles. "You can be my sous chef."

"I'd love to."

She opens the refrigerator. "Now let's see what my son has. Beer. Milk. Eggs. Lunchmeat." Then she opens the pantry door. "Bread. Cereal. Ramen noodles. Not much to work with, is there?"

My phone buzzes, and I see it is Adam. "This is your son."

"Oh good."

I read his text. *Sorry I'm so late. How's my mom?*

Your mom is great. We're having a good time.

I'll be home at seven-thirty. Thanks so much.

Can't wait to see you.

A red heart pops on my screen and I send him one back.

"Kathy, Adam says he'll be home at seven-thirty."

"That limits our choices on what to prepare." She opens the pantry. "First thing I'm going to do tomorrow is take Adam to the grocery store."

"I've got an idea. Why don't we move this party to my place? I've got a fully stocked kitchen and lots of things to choose from in the fridge and pantry."

"And more wine?" She winks.

"Oh yes."

"What are we waiting for? Let's go."

"Let me send a text to your son so he'll know where to go when he comes home." I type quickly. *We'll be at my apartment. Your mom wants to cook us dinner.*

Sounds good.

His mom and I walk out the door to my place.

Once inside, she says, "This is so beautiful. I need to take you back to Missouri with me. I could use your help decorating."

I grin. "Do you have wine in Missouri?"

She laughs. "Yes. In fact, I've been to the winery in Branson."

"Then perhaps I could come during one of the university's breaks."

"I would love that. You and Adam could drive together. That way you could meet his Pop."

I'm not sure that would be a good idea, but I don't say so. I've had my fill of bigots in my life. And if I met the man, I'd probably tell him so.

I take her into the kitchen. "First things first. I have a Malbec that I want you to taste."

"I've never had Malbec, but if you recommend it I will be happy to try it."

"Awesome. Make yourself at home, Kathy. Not only is *mi casa su casa*, but *mi concina es su concina.*"

"You speak Spanish?"

"Not really. I dated a guy who was from Argentina once and picked up a few things." I think about Miguel and how closeted and conflicted he was. Shortly after we got together he no longer felt shame about being gay. Now he's happily married with his husband in San Antonio.

As Kathy checks out my pantry and fridge, I open a bottle and fill two glasses for us.

"This is the most organized kitchen I've ever seen," she says, taking one of the glasses from me.

"Though I've never been diagnosed with OCD, I have been accused of it more than a few times."

"If this is the result of a little touch of OCD, then I want some." I laugh. "Your son said almost the exact same thing."

"What can I say? He's a little like me, too." She sips the wine. "This is wonderful."

"I'm glad." I lift the glass to my lips and taste the Malbec. "It's one of my favorites."

"This would pair perfectly with my spaghetti sauce."

"I love spaghetti."

"So does Adam, but my sauce takes six hours to make." She snaps her fingers. "We could cheat."

"Cheat?"

She pulls out a jar of sauce and a can of diced tomatoes from my pantry. "Yep. You have everything I need for my cheat sauce. Not quite as good but it will do in a pinch. You have fresh garlic."

"I do."

"Perfect. It only takes twenty minutes to make, but you can't tell Adam. It will be our little secret."

"You got a deal." I really am enjoying spending time with Adam's mom. In a way she reminds me of Malcolm. She's upbeat and positive just like he was. "How about I turn on some music for us, Kathy?"

"That would be great."

She pulls out some of my pots and places them on the stove.

I sync my phone with my stereo. "This is from three friends of mine who also live here. They call themselves Red Shimmer."

One of their songs starts to play.

She fills the pot and adds some spices. "I like their sound. Very nice. Has Adam met them?"

"Actually, they helped unload the truck the day he moved in. Everyone helped." I place my glass on the counter and salute her. "Sous chef reporting for duty, chef. What do you need me to do?"

She laughs. "How about you get the water boiling for the spaghetti first."

We are like a well-oiled machine in my kitchen. I can't remember when I had so much fun cooking before. The wine. The music. Laughing. It's a perfect recipe for a good time.

After a bit, she dips a spoon in the sauce. "Taste this, Oliver."

"Mmm. I love it."

She grabs a clean spoon and tastes the sauce herself. She shakes her head. "It still needs something, I think."

"Really? The seasoning is spot on to me. It couldn't be any better."

She takes a sip of her wine and then pours the rest into the pot. "That should make it perfect." She giggles.

I grab the bottle of Malbec, which is now almost empty. "Another glass, Kathy?"

"No. I've had plenty. That's why I put the rest of mine in the sauce. I can't feel my cheeks right now."

I laugh.

She places her empty glass in the dishwasher. "How long before Adam gets here?"

"Ten minutes."

"We better put the pasta in the water and the garlic bread in the oven."

"I'll handle the bread." I grab the baking sheet with the bread and open the oven door.

"And I'll handle the spaghetti." She places the pasta into the pot of boiling water next to the sauce.

My phone buzzes.

"It's Adam, again," I tell her, feeling excited that I'm about to see him. "Hey. You almost here?"

"Almost," he answers. "How's my mom?"

"Great. She's just like you said she would be."

"Oliver, thank you so much for doing this for me. I owe you."

I smile, seeing his mom start to set the table. "I've never had a better afternoon. We opened the bottle of wine that was on your counter and we've been getting to know each other ever since. You're very lucky to have such a wonderful mother."

"I know I am," he says.

"I love the story about you learning to skate when you were seven."

"Oh God." He laughs. "I better hurry or she'll tell all my secrets."

"Please hurry. I can't wait to dive into the meal she's made for us. Spaghetti."

"Mmm. My favorite. She's a great cook. You'll love her food."

"I know I will. I can't wait to see you."

"I can't wait to see you either, Oliver."

I click off the phone and turn to Adam's mom. "He's almost here."

She nods and we finish preparing the meal.

Ten minutes later, my doorbell rings.

I open the door and see Adam in his uniform looking good enough to eat.

"Hey," he says smiling.

"Hi."

Without another word, Adam rushes past me to his mom.

He wraps her in his arms and swings her around. "I'm so glad you're here, mom."

"Me, too. I missed you."

"I missed you, too." He glances at the table. "Wow. This looks and smells delicious."

"Let's eat," she says.

We sit and I pour Adam a glass of wine.

"Thanks, buddy."

Buddy? Shit. Here we go again.

"Would you mind passing the garlic bread to me?" I ask him.

"Here you go, buddy."

There's that word again.

"Mom, this is amazing."

133

"Your son is right, Kathy. Delicious." I take another bite. "I've never had better spaghetti."

She smiles. "It was the wine I added at the last."

Adam finishes his glass in two gulps. He seems a little unsettled.

"May I have some more wine?" he asks me.

"Of course." I refill his glass.

"Thanks, buddy." He turns to his mother. "I'm thinking about getting season passes to the Dallas Cowboys for me and Oliver. What do you think of that?"

"Sounds like a good idea to me if that's what you two want."

"It would be a good time for male bonding, don't you think, buddy?"

Damn it. "Sure. Why not?" Adam needs to be honest with his mother instead of pretending to be something he's not. He's never asked me if I like football. I do, but he's never asked. He's trying to act all macho. And it's pissing me off.

The longer the meal goes on and each time he says "buddy" and tries to turn up the testosterone, I get more and more angry. I try to keep my cool, but I know my agitation is showing on my face because Adam's eyes keep darting back and forth from his mom to me.

Adam holds up his empty glass again. "May I have another, Oliver?"

Unable to contain my anger any longer, I burst out, "It's about time you starting calling me by my name and not *buddy*,"

Adam looks stunned. "I didn't mean to upset you, Oliver. I swear."

"I know you didn't, but this macho crap has to go. It's time to be honest. Hell, your mother knows you don't act like a macho asshole. Tell her the truth."

"You're right. It's just that..." He glances at his mother and back at me. "It's difficult to say, but I know it needs to be said." He turns back to her. "Mom, I'm not who you think I am."

"Honey, you're exactly who I think you are."

"No. You don't understand. I've been living a lie. I'm gay."

"Yes, you're gay. I know." She smiles. "I've known for some time."

"You have?" His eyes widened.

"Yes. I have." With tears in her eyes, she reaches for his hand and mine and places them together. "Did you think that would bother me? Nothing has changed. You're the same wonderful son I've always been so proud of. I love you just the way you are."

Adam gets up and wraps his arms around his mother. "I love you, mom."

Chapter 17

I quietly leave Adam and his mom, realizing they need a moment alone. I step out on my patio with a fresh glass of wine, smiling. Like Kathy, I can't feel my cheeks either.

My mind drifts back to when I came out to my parents. I'm overwhelmed with emotions. How I wish it could have been like this for me. Adam shared his truth with his mom and she accepted him fully. But it wasn't like this for me. Not even close.

I no longer feel sorry for myself. Those days are behind me. What happened made me who I am today. Malcolm helped me to learn to let go of the past and to start looking to the future.

God, I miss him.

Adam joins me on the patio. "You."

"Me?"

He wraps his arms around me and presses his lips to mine. I melt into his embrace. I grab the back of his head, pulling him in tighter. I love tangling my tongue with his.

When he releases me, I'm warm all over.

"I feel like a weight has been lifted off my shoulders, Oliver. And you did this. You."

"No, Adam. You did this. You and your mom."

"She's known for some time. I still can't believe it." He kisses me again.

God, I would die a happy man if I could just taste his lips until my last breath. Forget eating, or sleeping, or anything else. I just want to kiss him again and again until my lips are throbbing for more.

"Adam, where's your mom?"

"I sent her back to my place with my key. She's exhausted from the drive and wants to get to bed. I think it might have just been an excuse to let you and me have a little time alone."

"It probably was," I say, realizing once again how much alike she and I are.

"Mom didn't want to leave a mess, but I told her you and I would be the cleanup crew." His eyes lock on mine and I feel a hot shiver move up and down my spine. "That was my excuse to get you all to myself."

I place my hands on his shoulders. "That's very devious of you, but I can be devious, too." I devour his mouth, sending my tongue past his lips. He tastes better than the wine. Our kiss deepens and I wrap my arms around his neck.

He pulls me in tight. His muscled body is rock solid, which adds an extra level of excitement.

When he starts kissing and sucking on my neck, I feel my pulse burning in my veins. I'm on fire with want. I've been dreaming about this moment since I shared Ramen noodles with him in his apartment. Hell, even before that when he dropped the box and interrupted Malcolm's memorial. I haven't been able to think about anything else. *Anyone else.*

"God, you look sexy in this uniform, but I'd like to see what's underneath."

When his eyes widen, I feel my gut tighten. Am I going too fast with him? Why the hell did I let him know I wanted him naked? Because, damn it, I do want him naked. I want him in my bed. Still, maybe he likes to take things nice and slow, especially after that guy cheated on him.

"You sound like you're starved for sex, Oliver." He grins

wickedly and then brushes his lips lightly against mine. "I sure am hungry to be with you. How about you? Are you hungry for me?"

"Damn right I am." Crazed with desire, I start unbuttoning his shirt. Once the last button slips out, my eyes are rewarded with the most perfectly sculpted chest I've ever seen. "Wow." I run my hands over his pecs down to his six-pack. "God, your body is amazing. Perfection."

He smiles. "Thanks to training annually for the Corp's PFT, physical fitness test. I still train every day, even though I don't have to any longer."

"Please keep it up, especially if this is the result." I play with his nipples and start feeling my cock stir in my jeans. The promise of sex has never felt like this before. Usually, my mind wanders, slipping in and out of the moment. But what is this unexplainable feeling I'm having with Adam? I'm fully present, in the here and now, totally engaged.

"Fair is fair. Now my turn." He pulls my black T-shirt over my head. "My God, you look good. You're really ripped."

I love hearing his praise. "Thanks to the university's gym and a terrific trainer."

"I've got to see more." Adam's voice rumbles over my skin as he moves his hands over my naked torso, stirring up my sexual desires.

"I'm so turned on. I've got to see more of you, too. But let's take this inside. Even though my patio has a privacy fence, my neighbors can catch a glimpse of it from their second-story windows."

"Not into exhibition, sweetheart?" He chuckles. "Me either, but I know for a fact that Unit E is vacant. And since our wonderful trio, Red Shimmer, has a gig tonight, I know they aren't home."

"You're bad." I'm crazy with his wicked spontaneity.

"Or is it the outdoors you're afraid of, Mr. President?" he asks

I lean down and lick his nipple. "I love the outdoors, Marine. Last one naked has to do the dishes." I kick off my shoes.

"So this is a competition, is it?" Adam unbuckles his belt and pulls it through the loops of his pants before tossing it to the ground.

"No, but I'm going to win," I say, pulling off my socks. What is it about him that puts me so at ease? There's a playful side to Adam that fascinates me. It's just one of the sides of his personality that I adore. When I place my jeans and underwear on one of the patio chairs, I see he's still wearing his pants. "Done. I win. This is Oliver Lancaster's naked body on display." I grin.

"I'm crazy about your naked body. You look incredible." He doesn't move to take off his last article of clothing. *His pants.*

And then it hits me that he's holding back because of his artificial leg. Is he worried I'll think less of him? Or is it just difficult for him to show the damage that bomb in Afghanistan did to his body?

I hold his hands, wanting to take this next step with him more than anything. I *need* to take this next step with him even though it scares me because I've never felt so strongly about any man before. Besides, I sense he needs this, too. "It's okay, Adam. Everything will be okay." I kiss him, hoping to remove any doubt he has. "Please. Let me see you."

He's hesitant. "Honestly, I'm nervous about letting you see. I don't want you to be disappointed in the way I look."

"You could never disappointment me, sweetheart."

He's the first man I've ever called *sweetheart.* Putting my arms around him and squeezing his hand, I lead him inside, up the stairs to my bedroom.

We stand next to my bed, and I kiss him gently. "It's going to be all right. I promise. Just trust me."

"I do trust you, but—"

I press my lips to Adam's again, trying to reassure him.

This moment is so intimate. I feel my heart pounding in my chest. I've never felt like this before with any other man. Sex has always been just that—sex. A means to an end. Only a physical act to get some brief pleasure from. Keeping my feelings, my emotions, my most inner thoughts locked away during sex are things I had to learn to survive. But being with Adam I can't. Could this be love I'm feeling for him? What do I know about love? I do know I don't want any other man touching him and I can't imagine another man ever touching me again.

I slowly pull his pants and black boxers down until they are down at his ankles, which reveals not only his cock, but also the place where the remainder of his right leg ends and his prosthetic begins.

"I'm surprised that you don't seem repulsed." Adam's eyes well up. "Or is it just that wishful thinking on my part?"

"What are you talking about? Don't be crazy."

"Crazy? I've been through this before." He closes his eyes and lets out a long sigh. "Maybe you're just trying to spare my feelings. Maybe you're just being the nice, wonderful man I'm falling in love with." He opens his eyes and stares at me. "A broken body is all I have to offer, Oliver. If you want to end this I will understand."

"End this? We're just beginning. I don't want to end anything." I kneel down and explore both of his legs, the flesh and the prosthetic. "I'm looking at the pinnacle of male beauty. Touching and seeing what that horrible bomb left of your right leg, I'm even more in awe of you. Lesser men would have given up, but not you, Adam. Not *my* Marine. You pushed through so much difficulty until you could walk again. Hell, not just walk. Run. I remember that day we both ran to the rally." I look up and lock my eyes with his. "You're so strong, so heroic. I want you more than any man I've ever wanted before. Do I understand my feelings? No. I just know I have them for you."

He pulls me up to my feet until we're face to face. "I can't believe how lucky I am."

Again we kiss. There's urgency on our lips and hunger in our mouths. I can feel the pulse in my veins getting hotter and hotter.

I slowly inch my tongue from his neck to his nipples down to his abs. "You like this?"

"God, yes." He runs his hands through my hair. "I love it."

As I kiss his navel, swirling my tongue inside, I take hold of his cock.

He groans, which thrills me. I'm on fire for him.

With my hand still on my cock, I lightly squeeze his heavy balls with my other hand. "God, you've got a monster between your legs, sweetheart. I can't wait to taste you." *Sweetheart.* There's that word again. It seems so natural to call Adam that.

"I can't wait to feel your lips on me," he says in a lusty tone.

His words make me sizzle.

After enjoying his astonishing skills at kissing, I want to pleasure him by giving him oral sex. I drag my tongue up and down his cock and then I lick the tip.

"Damn. That feels so good, baby." He holds me by the hair, urging me to continue.

I bob up and down his cock, reveling at the impact I'm having on him. Hearing his breathing speed up, I recognize he's getting close, causing my desire for him to multiply and surge.

When he comes inside my mouth, I'm elated. God, this connection with him is something new and overwhelming.

"Sweetheart, that was off-the-charts incredible." He pulls me back to my feet and gently ushers me onto my back on the bed. He kisses me and then says, "My turn to taste you, honey."

I smile. "I'd like that, sweetheart."

He sits on the edge of my bed and starts to detach his prosthetic leg.

I sit up next to him, grabbing his hand. "Let me do that. Please."

"You amaze me, Oliver Lancaster."

"Show me how."

"It's easy." Adam guides my hands and we remove his artificial leg together.

Once detached, I place it on the floor next to the bed. I touch what's left of his right leg. "Does it hurt?"

"It gets sore if I over do, which causes me to limp. Other than that, it doesn't hurt, except for phantom pain sometimes. That's where the brain tries to tell me my right leg is still there." Adam grins. "But enough about that, sweetheart." He crawls on top of me, kissing me into a state of delirium.

As he slides down my body, his hot breath raises my temperature. I'm out of control and relishing in the sensations he's bringing out in me. When I feel his mouth on my cock, a moan escapes my lips. There's no going back for me now. None. I'm all in, God help me. He's the one I want. The only one.

He devours my cock, and I claw his shoulders, wrapping my legs around him.

I'm mad and ravenous. "Don't stop. So close. So damn close."

I groan, and every cell in my body engages in the volcanic explosion he's giving me.

He moves up the bed and wraps his arms around me. "Fair warning, sweetheart. I love to cuddle."

I smile. "I never have before, but with you I'm sure I'll love it. God, that was wonderful, astonishing, mind-blowing, marvelous…I need more adjectives, Adam."

He laughs. "Do you have a dictionary I can go get us?"

"Yes, I have a dictionary." I kiss him. "But you're not leaving my bed, Marine. Not a chance." I gaze into his eyes, knowing he's ruined me for other men. "Seriously, there's just no words to describe how I feel and what you do to me. I don't know what to say."

"Then let me try. You mean the world to me." He kisses my forehead. "After I lost my leg, I got through the rehab and counseling, but I wasn't in good shape. I wanted my old life back, my old body. There hasn't been a day since the bombing that I haven't hated how things turned out, until now. *Until you.* Since I met you I've stopped feeling sorry for myself, feeling lesser. But it wasn't just about my leg. In a funny sort of way hiding the fact that I had lost my leg was just like hiding my sexuality—just another closet I disappeared into. But you, Oliver, showed me that I've been missing so much. There's so much life to be lived. And love to be felt." He traces my jawline with his hands. "I love you."

Everything inside me wants to say it back to him. They're just three little words. It should be easy. Just open my mouth and let it out. It's the truth after all. But how can I tell him? He doesn't know who I really am, what I've done. He deserves so much better than me. So instead I just kiss him, praying it's enough of a response to keep him with me for just a little longer, though it's breaking my heart knowing this has to end.

Chapter 18

My arms and legs are wrapped around a sleeping Adam. I can't sleep. He told me that he loved me, but I couldn't say it back. God, I wish I could. But for now I don't want to drift off. I need to fully enjoy the feeling of having him lying next to me in my bed. *Yes, Adam, I love to cuddle now.* How long can I let this go on? The longer I do the more devastated I will be. I'm a selfish bastard. What about Adam's feelings?

I need to let you go but I just can't.

He's everything I could want. Strong. Heroic. Caring. Brave. And he's now living in his truth. He's not imprisoned in the closet anymore. He wants to tell his grandfather as soon as he can, though he's a little worried how that will go. I don't know the man but after hearing what Adam told me I know there's a pretty good chance it could go badly. I vow silently to be ready to help Adam no matter how it turns out.

I inhale his scent. God, he smells so good.

I hear a loud bang and the bed starts to shake.

"Take cover!" Adam starts flailing his arms and accidently hits me directly in the nose with his elbow.

"Adam, wake up." Blood runs out of my nose. As the bed continues to shake, I yell, "It's just another earthquake!"

"Oh my God, Oliver. You've been shot." Adam rolls on top of me, clearly trying to give me cover from an unseen enemy soldier.

"Adam. Adam." My voice rises, trying to get his attention. "I haven't been shot. We're in my apartment. Wake up. Please wake up."

After the shaking stops, he moves off of me, sits on the side of the bed, and hangs his head. "I'm so sorry. I haven't had one of these dreams in a few months." He grabs his prosthetic from the floor and puts it on. "I don't know what triggers them."

"I have a pretty good idea why it happened." I reach for some tissues off of my nightstand and bring them up to my bleeding nose. "You just went through another difficult experience. The shooting at the university likely caused the memories from what happened to you in Afghanistan to resurface. And you haven't had much sleep. And don't forget that we both drank a little too much wine. And finally, we just went through another earthquake, which started the dream in the first place."

"Earthquakes in Dallas?" He raises his head and looks directly at me. "Oh God, Oliver. Your nose is bleeding. I did that to you, didn't I?" He leans in close. "Did I break it? Are you okay?"

"I'm fine. No, you didn't break it, and this isn't the first nose-bleed I've ever had." I grin, hoping to ease his concerns. "I'm tough. I'll survive."

"Can I get you some ice?" His anxious tone actually makes me feel good. "What can I do to help you?"

"I think it stopped. Just let me go wash it off and I'll be as good as new." I walk into the bathroom with Adam right beside me, staring at me with a worried look.

I finish cleaning up. "See. Good as new, just like I said."

He hugs me. "I'm so sorry."

"It's all right." I kiss him. "I bet that was over a 3.5 earthquake."

"I had no idea that Dallas had earthquakes." His eyes are still wide and locked on me.

"We didn't until recently." I decide to keep on talking about the

146

earthquake just to try to get his mind off of his nightmare. "Some people think it's because of the fracking in the area, but no one knows for certain. Still, it's a likely explanation. The scientific community is still trying to determine the cause. That last one was pretty big compared to the previous ones. I'm sure it's causing some foundation issues around the area. I hope Mockingbird Place didn't get any damage. I'll need to check with Sarah and Martha about getting earthquake insurance."

Adam grabs my hand and squeezes it. "Oliver, I was right back in Afghanistan. God, it seemed so real. When I saw you bleeding I thought I'd lost you."

"I'm right here. Safe. In your arms. We're both safe."

We hold onto each other until I know he's feeling better and the nightmare has completely vanished. "We're both wide awake now with no chance of falling back to sleep."

We go back into my bedroom. He puts his uniform back on.

I grab my robe. "Why don't I make us a pot of coffee?"

"What time is it?"

"Five-thirty."

"I better skip the coffee. I should get back to my place. My mom usually wakes up around six." He smiles and kisses me. "Though I'm not ready to leave you, I really should check on her."

I kiss him back. "Go before I try to change your mind because I do agree that you need to check on your mom. She did drive all the way from Missouri to see you."

Arm in arm, we walk to my front door.

Once again, he pulls me in close. "I love you, Oliver."

And once again, I smile but don't say anything back.

He kisses me tenderly and then he leaves.

I step out to watch him walk to his door. He turns and waves at me. After he goes inside, I step back into my apartment and shut the door.

"Why can't you say it back, Oliver Lancaster? What's so tough about telling him how you feel?"

I love him. I know I do, but I'm not good enough for him. He's a hero and I'm damaged goods. If he knew what I had done, he wouldn't have anything to do with me.

I walk into the kitchen and start making coffee. Once I pour myself a cup, my phone rings. It's Adam.

"Did you forget something?" I ask him.

"Not a thing, handsome. Mom was already up when I got here. She wants to cook you and me breakfast."

"That sounds wonderful. Let me grab a quick shower and I'll be right over." I click off the phone and rush to my bathroom.

Turning on the water, I realize there isn't any reason for me to tell Adam about what happened when I first arrived in Dallas. No one knows about it but me now that Malcolm is gone. Besides, Adam and I are just at the beginning of things. This is only dating. It's not serious. It can't be serious. *Really? Who am I trying to kid?* Having breakfast with a guy and his mother *is* very serious. I know I love him. God help me because I can't help myself. I must see him. I'll worry about the consequences later.

I step out of the shower and see another text from Adam.

Mom wondered if you have syrup.

I do. I'll bring it.

Or I could come get it and steal a kiss.

I grin and type back, *I'll be waiting.*

I wrap a towel around my waist and hear my doorbell ring. I laugh, glad that he is so anxious to return.

I open the door and instead of finding Adam I see Trent standing on my porch. "Come inside. What are you doing here so early?"

"I can't, Oliver. I need to get home but I wanted to see you first to find out about Candy. It was all over the news in London—she and the vice president. I drove straight here from the airport." Trent wraps his arms around me. "She is going to be okay, isn't she?"

I know how sensitive and caring Trent can be. "She's fine. The doctors say she will make a full recovery."

"That's wonderful news. And how are *you* doing? You've been through so much."

"Actually, I'm better than I've been in a long time."

"I'm so glad." Trent smiles. "I hope I didn't wake you."

"You didn't. I'm about to have an early breakfast with my new boyfriend and his mother."

"Oh. I'm so happy for you." Trent grabs me and kisses me on the cheek. "Maybe this one will be the right one for you. I'm exhausted so I better get going. I'd like to see Candy if they are allowing her visitors."

"They are and I know she'd loved to see you."

"What hospital is she at?"

"Parkland. Room 772."

"Thanks, *buddy*. I'll see you later." Trent hugs me again and then leaves.

I still hate that word. I glance at Adam's front door, wondering why he hasn't come for the syrup yet. Probably playing sous chef for his mother.

I rush back to my bedroom to get dressed. I can't wait another second before I see *my* Marine.

Chapter 19

Holding the syrup bottle, I ring Adam's doorbell and hear one of the familiar Mozart pieces begin to play. I smile, remembering how proud Malcolm was of his doorbell. I hope Adam appreciates it.

Adam's mom opens the door, looking upset.

"What's wrong?" I ask her. "Is Adam all right?"

"No, Oliver," she says in a very serious tone. "Adam stepped out to go to your place to get the syrup, saw you kissing that man, came back, got his keys, and then left."

My heart sinks. "Oh my God, Kathy. That was just a friend who had heard about the shooting while he was in London. Trent just wanted to make sure that Candy was doing well."

"I knew there had to be a simple explanation, but my son wasn't in any frame of mind to hear that from me or anyone else for that matter."

"Damn. I need to talk to him. I can understand why he feels that way after what he saw. I was only in a towel and someone he doesn't know hugs me and kisses me on the cheek."

"On the cheek?" She shakes her head. "He thought it was on the mouth. Come in and let me pour you a cup of coffee."

"Let me send him a text first." I hand her the syrup bottle and pull out my phone. "This is just a big misunderstanding."

Please, Adam. Let me explain.

I hear a buzzing sound and turn to find Adam's phone on the coffee table. "Shit. Shit. Shit. He left his phone. I feel so frustrated and helpless. What can I do to fix this, Kathy?"

"Don't worry. Adam loves to drive when he's upset or needs to think things out."

"I know. He told me." My insides are churning. I keep glancing out the window, hoping to see him walking up the sidewalk. I hate ever second that passes that Adam's not here. "Where is he?"

She hands me a cup. "He'll be back before you know it. Let's sit down."

"I just can't sit down right now." I start pacing. "He thinks I betrayed him."

"But you didn't," she says softly.

"He doesn't know that."

"Oliver, I've been around a long time. I know this seems like a crisis but it isn't. As soon as he walks in that door you can straighten this out."

"I just hate this waiting."

"Me, too." She smiles. "We are alike, you and I. But I know my son. If he didn't care about you so much he wouldn't have stormed out of here. You matter to him, Oliver."

"And he matters to me. Much more than I realized. I love him, Kathy."

"I already knew that, sweetheart. I could tell by the look in your eyes."

"But I haven't told him."

"But you should tell him." She points to the window. "And here comes Adam now. I'll give you two some privacy." She hurries up the stairs.

The door opens.

And then Adam sees me. "What the hell are you doing here?" Apparently his drive didn't cool him off. "There's not going to be breakfast. At least not with you."

"Will you just let me explain? Please."

"How can you explain something I saw with my own eyes, Oliver? Who is he?"

"Just a friend. I swear."

"Don't give me that shit." He angrily tosses his keys into the bowl by the door. "I saw you two kissing."

"Trent only kissed me on the cheek."

He frowns. "I know what I saw. On the mouth."

"No. You must have seen the back of his head, Adam." I'm so frustrated that he won't believe me. "And you want to know why he kissed me *on the cheek* in the first place? I just told him I was eating breakfast with my boyfriend and he was happy for me."

"So that's why your *friend* came over at six in the morning? To congratulate you on having a boyfriend? Really? You expect me to believe that?"

"Yes, I do expect you to believe that—to believe me. You say you love me and yet you don't trust me. You don't even give me a chance to explain everything. You came in here ready for a fight. Fine. If it's a fight you want then it's a fight you'll get." I step right in front of him and stare directly into his eyes. "Listen to me, Marine, and listen good. Here's what happened. Trent came over to find out about Candy. He just flew in from a business trip and drove straight from DFW to find out if I was okay. And before you ask, yes, Trent and I dated. Even though we broke it off, we are still friends."

Adam sighs. "I guess I mistook—"

"I'm not done talking."

"You've got the floor."

"You're damn right I've got the floor. You told me that part of the reason you stayed in the closet was because of the cheating you saw from gays you knew in the military. Adam, you don't know all the gays in the military. I'm sure not all of them cheat, nor do all civilian gays. Guess, what? I don't cheat. I never have."

"Oliver, I know you wouldn't. I'm just an idiot." He moves to pull me into his arms, but I step back.

"Damn it, do you really want this to work? Us to work?"

"Of course I do."

"Then you need to trust me." I pause for a moment, gathering my thoughts. "But why should you when I haven't told you everything? I can't really blame you for doubting me." I've run out of steam and my frustration at him is gone. "I tell everyone they should live in their truth. No regrets. But I've built an invisible closet of my own—a cage of shame that I haven't been able to escape."

"What is it? What could be so bad that you haven't been able to share this with anyone?"

I'm so scared to tell this part of me that has been hidden for so long. What if he thinks less of me? What if he can't handle it? What if I lose him? But I must tell him. No more secrets.

"Only Malcolm knew this about me." I take a deep breath as my mind dredges up those horrible memories. "I told you about coming to Dallas when I was fifteen. What I left out was the six months I was here before I met Malcolm. After getting off the bus, I ran out of money in less than a month. I had nowhere to go, no friends, no money. I ended up sleeping in a dumpster behind one of the bars. I was desperate, Adam. I knew if I went to the authorities they would just ship me back to my parents and I would go back to that awful ranch.

"One night this man came up to me claiming to be a photographer. He told me that I looked like Brad Pitt and offered me money to model for him. I was so excited. I hadn't eaten in two or three days. Hell, I don't remember how long it was. I just know I was starving."

"Oh my God, Oliver. He was a pedophile, wasn't he?"

"Yes, but more than that. The bastard used me and other boys he took from the streets to make money for him. It was quite the racket. He would feed us, fill us with drugs, and shove us out to dirty old men. Once a boy got too old or too used up or out of his mind from the drugs, the motherfucker would push the kid back onto the streets to die."

I see Adam's eyes welling up.

"You deserve to know everything about me. I was a teenage prostitute, Adam. A hooker at fifteen. I hated myself, hated what I was doing. I thought God was punishing me. I wanted to kill myself and would have if Malcolm hadn't found me.

"I was supposed to meet a John at the corner of Cedar Springs and Throckmorton. That's where most of the gay bars are located. But the man never showed. I knew if I came back without money I would be beaten. So I started flirting with every man who passed by. No one paid any attention to me. Why would they? I was dirty and high and so skinny. I knew the bastard was days away from kicking me out. A thousand times before I'd thought about jumping in front of a car to end it all. I moved to the edge of the sidewalk and waited. A white van, which reminded me of that fucking vehicle that took me out of my parents' home to the ranch, raced my direction. At that very moment I found the courage to step off the curb, but a hand pulled me back and saved me. Malcolm's hand.

"He smiled at me and said, 'Better be more careful, young man. You almost got yourself killed.' Malcolm bought me a burger and then took me to his place. I believed I'd found my John for the night.

"His place...*this* place...looked like a palace to me: so clean, beautiful, everything in order just where it was supposed to be— quite the opposite of the shack where I was living with three other boys and our bastard pimp. Soiled black from years of neglect and misuse, three mattresses, side by side, covered the grimy floor. I tried to clean the disgusting toilet once, but the bastard beat me yelling, 'You think you're too good for my home, you little prick.' Even though I was repulsed at my living conditions, I never picked up a rag again.

"Malcolm led me to his bathroom, gave me fresh towels, and left me a clean robe to put on. I took him up on his offer to wash my clothes. When he said I could stay in his guest room for as long as I liked, I thought he was just another pimp, only cleaner. Up until that night, everything I was given came with a very high price. And so I wondered what Malcolm would demand from me.

"Before I got in the shower I took a long hard look at my reflection in the mirror. I was a total wreck. My hair was matted and filthy. Bruises were on my arms and legs. When the warm water hit my skin, I felt like I'd died and gone to heaven. It was incredibly invigorating. I washed my hair at least four or five times before I was satisfied it was clean. I scrubbed my skin over and over until it was smooth and all the ground-in dirt that accumulated over the past several weeks was gone. That shower was so strange to me, like a baptism. I felt pure and clean. I thought this wonderful feeling was only going to last for a moment because Malcolm was still waiting for me on the other side of the door. Once I left his bathroom, I assumed I would have to return to my dirty life as a little whore. I stayed in there for at least thirty minutes. Malcolm knocked on the door, and I tensed. I expected he wanted sex. I was wrong. He was just checking on me.

"When I came out of the bathroom in the robe he'd given me, I found him sitting in the kitchen with two slices of chocolate cake and a glass of milk for me and a cup of coffee for him. I was thrilled. I hadn't had any sweets since I started working the streets. I remember when I finished my cake, I reached out and touched Malcolm's hand, asking him what he liked to do in the bedroom. He smiled, pulled his hand back, and told me that he liked to sleep in the bedroom. Then he asked me to help him clean up our dishes. I was stunned. I was used to men who wanted me for my body. He was geninunely interested in me. When we finished drying and putting up the dishes, Malcolm led me to his guest room. He handed me the remote to the television and said goodnight before heading to his room.

"I was shocked. No one had ever treated me like that before. At the time I actually thought he might be crazy. Imagine that.

"When I thought he was asleep, I went down the stairs as quietly as I could. I grabbed his Rolex, which I had noticed he had placed on his kitchen counter when we did the dishes, and headed to his front door.

"But Malcolm was waiting for me in his chair. He told me that he'd taken off his Rolex in front of me on purpose. And that's when he said, 'I'm going to give you two choices, young man.' He told me I could walk out his door with the Rolex. Malcolm said he wouldn't call the police if I did."

"What was the other choice?" Adam asks.

"I could give him back the Rolex and stay." I look at the watch on my wrist. "Thank God, I chose to stay. After he died, he left it to me. So now you know everything about me Adam. I care about you. I care about you so much." Tears stream down my face. "I've told you my truth. I don't want to lose you but I can understand if you want to break it off with me."

"Seems to me I have two choices. I can ask you to walk to that door and never come back. Or I can ask you to stay." Adam pulls me into his arms. "But I don't really have a choice, do I?" He presses his lips to mine, and I melt into him. "I'm in love with you. Please stay, Oliver. Stay with me now and forever."

I answer him with a kiss. "Forever."

Chapter 20

When Adam goes to the half bath to get some tissues for us, I wipe my eyes with my hands. I'm so elated. He heard the most horrible things about me and still he wants me.

His mom comes down the stairs.

"Oh, Oliver, I'm so sorry." Her eyes brim with tears of her own. "What can I do to help?"

"Help with what, Mom?" Adam runs to her. "What's wrong? Are you okay?"

I start laughing, realizing the confusion my tears have caused.

He turns to me and frowns. "Oliver, don't laugh. Can't you see she's upset about something?"

"Adam? You're here. You didn't leave again." His mom starts laughing with me. "I get it now. I didn't at first."

"What am I missing?" Adam asks. "What's so funny? First you are crying but now you're laughing."

"When I saw Oliver wiping his eyes and you weren't with him, I thought you two had ended it. So my eyes welled up. Now I realize Oliver's were happy tears. And all these tears have made me hungry. Are you two ready for breakfast yet?"

Adam puts his arm around her and reaches for my hand. "I'm starving. Let's eat."

"Give me a second to warm our meal back up," his mom says. "Would you two put on a fresh pot of coffee for us?"

Adam salutes his mother. "Yes, ma'am."

She and I grin.

And in a flash, she gets our food back on the table—sausage, eggs, biscuits and gravy, and pancakes.

When I take my first bite, I'm impressed. "Kathy, how in the world did you make this taste like you just made it instead of over an hour ago?"

She grins. "I've learned a few secrets over the years, Oliver."

"I thought I was a good cook, but now I realize I have a lot more to learn. Would you be willing to share your secrets with me?"

"Of course, sweetheart. I'd love to. Any old-fashioned cook knows my tricks. Besides, we can't have any secrets between us, can we?"

"You're right." I look at Adam, the man of my dreams.

"Would you like more coffee," he asks.

"Please."

"What about you, Mom?"

She nods.

After he fills our cups, I grab his hand. "I want to tell your mom what I told you. I want her to know my truth, my secrets."

Adam smiles. "I think you should, Oliver."

Having him next to me makes me feel safe and gives me courage.

"Kathy, this isn't easy for me to say."

"Oliver, no matter what it is, know it won't change how I feel about you."

"I believe you. I told your son my darkest secret, something I've been keeping hidden from everyone. I thought if people knew what I had done they would no longer want to be in my life. But Adam knows everything and he still wants me, wants us to be together."

"Oliver, of course he does," she says. "No matter what

happened to you doesn't change the fact that you are a wonderful, amazing young man."

I tell her about how I came out to my parents and them sending me to the ranch.

With tears streaming down her cheeks, she says, "Oh, you poor boy. I'm so sorry, Oliver. I wish I could have been there to help you."

"I'm glad you're here now, Kathy."

"Have you tried to reach out to your parents?" she asks. "Maybe they've changed."

"They haven't. I called them just last year to see if they might be able to accept me. A lot of time had passed. I was hopeful. My mother answered the phone. I said, 'This is Oliver.' And she answered, 'Oliver, who?' 'Your son Oliver, mother.' And she said, 'I don't have a son. My son is dead.' And then she hung up on me."

Kathy looks stricken. "How can a mother do that to her child?"

"In their eyes, I'm dead. I've been dead to my parents since I told them I was gay. That's why they sent me to the ranch. They didn't want me around. I thought the ranch was horrible, but I had no idea that it was going to get much worse." I continue telling her the whole story about my first six months in Dallas. Each detail that I share releases more and more of the weight of shame I've been carrying for so long. I feel free.

Her face darkens. "Hell isn't hot enough for that bastard who did that to you and the other boys."

"You sound like Malcolm. The good thing is that with his help and encouragement, I went to the police. The asshole was arrested and is still in prison to this day. The other three boys were rescued. That's when Malcolm founded Lifeline, an organization that helps homeless teens get food and shelter."

When I finish, I see she's still crying and so is Adam, which causes my own eyes to tear up. "Here we go again. I'll get the tissues this time."

Adam and his mom start laughing, and I join in.

She gets up and puts her arms around me. "My sweet Oliver.

You're not alone anymore. I'm your mom from now on. I'll even adopt you if you want me too."

"Mom, that won't work," Adam says with a grin. "We can't be brothers. I intend to marry this man."

"You do?" I'm surprised and happy.

"Damn right I do." He leans in and kisses me. "Now that I've found you I'm not letting you go."

Adam's phone buzzes. He looks at the screen and I see his eyes narrow.

"Mom, it's Granddad. I'll put it on speaker."

I can tell Adam is thinking about how he's going to come out to his grandfather. No matter what happens, I want to be by his side when he does to support him.

"How's my favorite grandson?" His grandfather has a much more pleasant voice than I expected.

"I'm your *only* grandson, Granddad, unless there's something you aren't telling me," Adam answers smiling. He leans my direction and in a low tone says, "It's something we've said to each other since I was a child."

"Adam, I'm so proud of you. Everyone in town is. I keep kicking myself for not coming with your mom to see you. I don't know what got into me. The old homestead will be fine without me, and I got Joe…you do remember Joe, don't you? Anyway, I got Joe to agree to take care of Buster."

"Buster is our dog," Adam informs me. "A ten-year-old German Shepherd. When are you coming?"

"I bought a one-way ticket to Dallas. Haven't been in a plane since Uncle Sam flew me back from Vietnam. I'll be there tomorrow morning."

"Looking forward to it." Adam takes a deep breath.

Looks like he's going to get his chance tomorrow to come out to his grandfather. I grab his hand and squeeze, letting him know that he won't be alone when he does.

"Tell your mom I'll drive back with her."

"I'm here, Pop," she says. "That sounds great. I'd like the company."

"Me, too, Kathy. Can you believe our boy?" The man's voice shakes a little. "Adam would be so proud of his son."

I realize that Adam must have been named after his father.

Adam's grandfather shares his flight information and says, "Well, I better get packing."

"I love you, Granddad. You're my favorite grandfather."

"I'm your only grandfather, unless there's something you're not telling me."

Adam laughs. "What could I not be telling you, Granddad?"

"You tell me, Adam. You tell me. I love you."

I grin. I can't help but like the man. He's got the same charming personality as his grandson.

"I love you, Kathy. I'll see you both tomorrow. This is going to be so much fun."

"I love you, too, Pop. See you soon."

I hope things go well tomorrow when Adam tells his grandfather he's gay, but I'm not holding my breath. Once a Marine, always a Marine. *Once a bigot, always a bigot?* It's true for my parents, but maybe it won't be true for his granddad. We'll just have to wait and see.

After Adam clicks off the phone, his mom says to him, "You okay?"

"Yeah, I just know I've got to tell him I'm gay and I don't have a clue how he's going to react."

She puts her arm around him. "Would you like me to call him? I could soften the blow."

Adam shakes his head and his eyes lock with mine. "No, Mom. This is my truth to share. Oliver showed me what true courage is all about. I'll tell Granddad."

I'm overwhelmed with emotion. "God, I'm so lucky to have you in my life, Adam Stockton."

"I love you, too, Oliver Lancaster."

"So formal," his mom says with a smile. "If it's formal you want then formal you'll get. And I, Katherine Marie Stockton are so proud of both my sons and I love them will all my heart."

Adam and I wrap her in our arms.

When we release her, her eyes widen. "Oh my goodness. I just thought of something. Where are we going to put Pop when he gets here, Adam? You only have the two beds."

"I guess I can sleep on the couch."

"Not a chance." I kiss him lightly on the lips. "You're sleeping at my place."

A text pops up on my phone's screen.

"It's from Martha," I tell him and Kathy.

Candy is doing great. Wondering if you could drop by her place to get her hairbrush and makeup case.

"I'm supposed to relieve Martha and Sarah from sitting with Candy at nine." I look at the clock on Adam's wall. 8:05 am. I stand and start clearing the table. "Damn. Time has gotten away from me. I had no idea it was this late."

Adam moves to the sink.

"Don't worry about the dishes, guys," Kathy says. "Adam, why don't you go with Oliver to see Candy? I'll handle the cleanup and then I'll call you and Oliver to see if Candy is up for a visit. I haven't had a chance to met her yet, but I'd like to."

"I'd like for you to meet her too," I say. "She's like a sister to me."

"Then she's definitely someone I must get to know."

"Are you sure you don't mind, Mom?" Adam asks. "We haven't had much time to talk."

"We'll have plenty of time to talk. I'm here for six more days." She smiles. "Go. Get out of here. I'll meet you at the hospital."

We walk out the front door and I send a text back to Martha. *I'll get Candy's things. Adam and I will be there soon.*

Chapter 21

At midnight, I dive into the pool and start my laps.

What a day it has been. Candy is getting stronger and stronger each hour. She was thrilled to see Adam and to meet his mom. Mom and Candy hit it off right away. The three of us stayed with Candy until Franki came back to relieve me of my shift. Candy stated she didn't need twenty-four-hour care from us. But when Franki said she wanted to stay anyway, Candy's eyes lit up.

I swear there's more going on between those two than they're letting on.

After we left the hospital, Adam and I took his mom to dinner to a fine-dining Mexican restaurant located downtown. We had such a blast, and I really loved it when Adam kept squeezing my leg under the table.

We just got back twenty minutes ago. Mom was all giggles when I said goodnight to her. She told us that she had too many margaritas and needed to go to bed. Adam took her back to his place with the promise to join me by the pool shortly.

I can't wait to spend some alone time with him.

I finish my laps and get out of the pool to dry off with the towel I brought. Certain that Adam won't swim, I don't want to get him wet when we sit on the bench. *Our bench.* The bench under Malcolm's tree.

I see Martha step out of her place and light a cigarette.

I move to the bench and she walks my direction.

"Franki just called S and me. Says Candy is doing amazing. Dr. Patterson says he might even release her a day early."

"I'm not surprised. She is a former Marine, after all."

Martha nods. "We were supposed to take the midnight shift but Franki says she wants to stay tonight."

"Again, not surprised. Those two have made a love connection I think. Besides, Candy doesn't want us hovering over her anymore. She doesn't mind visitors but says she's quite capable of taking care of herself now." When Adam's door opens, I'm shocked at what I see.

Adam is only wearing swimming trunks with a towel draped over his shoulder. His prosthetic is in clear view and he walks right up to Martha and me.

He leans over and gives Martha a kiss on the cheek. "How are you doing, pretty lady?"

"You good-looking devil, I'm doing just fine, especially since you called me pretty."

"Hey, handsome." He kisses me.

This is such a big difference in him. I wonder if he had too many margaritas like his mom. But then I remember he didn't have any since he was our driver today. I like this new side of Adam. I like it a lot.

"It looks like it's official," Martha says. "You two are a couple, right?"

"We are," Adam says in an emphatic tone. Then he sits down next to me and takes my hand. "And I'm going to marry him."

"You are?" I ask, smiling. "I don't remember you getting down on one knee."

"Don't worry. That's coming. Just waiting for the right time."

"Oh my God," she says, clapping her hands. "That's fantastic."

"I can't wait to see you and Sarah get married next Sunday," he says, standing and then walking to the side of the pool.

Then to my utter surprise, Adam sits down and removes his prosthetic leg.

"What are you doing?" I ask him.

He smiles. "I thought we were going to swim, Oliver."

I can't believe how much has changed since he shoved me out of his apartment after I saw his artificial legs. And now look at him— unashamed and full of life. He's the man of my dreams, the man I want to spend the rest of my life with.

"I'll see you boys later. I've got to go tell S the happy news."

Using his prosthetic as a crutch, Adam gets up, balances on his left leg, and then dives in.

When he comes up out of the water, he's laughing. "What are you waiting for, sweetheart? The water is great."

I leap from the bench, dive into the pool, and swim into his arms.

Our lips meet for one delicious kiss. We pull each other close and gaze into each other's eyes.

He grins. "Do you know what time it is, Oliver?"

"A little after midnight."

"Wrong." He laughs. "It's battle time." Suddenly, he pushes me away and begins splashing me like a maniac.

I dive under the water and grab him, pulling him below the surface. He wrestles free of my hold and swims away.

When I come up for air, he says, "So that's how it's going to be." He starts splashing me again. "You forget I'm a Marine. Get it? Marine. Water. The two go hand in hand."

"You started this battle, but I'm going to finish it." I splash him back, laughing my ass off.

We continue the war until Tony yells down from his bedroom window, "Do you mind, guys? Some of us are trying to sleep."

"Sorry, Tony." I turn to Adam, and in a much quieter tone say, "We better finish this battle at my place."

"Your place? That's the kind of war I like."

I grin. "Me, too. Home field advantage."

He swims to the edge of the pool and gets out with ease.

I join him and we both dry off.

Putting on his prosthetic, he says, "I love you so much."

My heart swells with joy. *Oliver, tell him how you feel. It's just three little words.*

He leans over and kisses me. "Do you mind giving me a hand to help me get up?"

"Sure thing." I stand and hold out my hand.

He's on his feet before I know it, and without warning, pushes me back in the pool.

"First one inside wins." He races to my door.

Laughing, I get out of the pool, grab my towel, and chase him. I feel like I'm a teenager again, not a twenty-one-year-old.

He shoots through my door several steps ahead of me. Locking it during my swim is something I've never done. Why should I? I can see my door from the pool. But right now I wish I had.

I sprint through my door, but there's no sign of Adam anywhere. "Where the hell are you, Marine?"

From my bedroom upstairs I hear him call down, "I win. Get your hot ass up here, Mr. President."

I fly up the stairs and into my bedroom to find Adam lying on my bed naked, stroking his cock.

Removing his prosthetic, he sends me that wicked grin that I can't resist. "Time for my reward, sweetheart. I won the battle."

My cock hardens, creating a tent of my trunks. "And what reward do you want, honey?"

"Slip out of those trunks," he says in a commanding tone that leaves me burning up with lust on the inside. "Then I'll tell you."

I smile and salute him. "Yes, sir." I'm out of my trunks and on top of him before you can say Yankee Doodle Dandy. Our hard cocks rub against each other.

Our mouths crash into each other like two freight trains colliding on a single track. There's nothing sweet or innocent or tender about this moment. This is blistering hot fierce frenzy. A wild primal passion, unleashed and unrelenting. Our hands and mouths crisscross over each other's bodies, touching and tasting lips and nipples and skin. I'm out of my mind with lust for him, out of control, and loving it.

"Tell me what you want, Marine." I devour his mouth, sending my tongue past his lips. "What reward do you want?"

His eyes are full of lust for me and that turns me on even more. "I want you, Oliver. I want to be inside you."

"I want that too," I confess. I've never had such an overwhelming desire for another man before. "More than anything."

I wrap my hands around his thick, hard cock and open my nightstand drawer, retrieving condoms and a bottle of lube. Keeping hold of him, I rip one of the little square packages open with my teeth. I place the condom against my lips and slide it down his shaft by swallowing him.

He groans. "Wow. Now that's the way to put on a condom."

"I thought you'd like that. Now to get my ass ready for this beast." I squeeze his cock and pop the top of the bottle of lube.

Adam puts his hand over mine. "Please. Let me."

Heat radiates through me and I feel my pulse in my cock. "Winner's choice."

I brush my lips over his and stretch out on my bed face down and spread eagle. As he begins applying the slick lubricant to my ass, I feel my toes curl. This is unfamiliar territory for me. Normally, I'm the top in the bedroom. I've bottomed before, a few times, but it has never been something I sought or craved. Right now, with him fingering my ass, there's nothing I want more than for him to be inside me. Being with Adam is exposing parts of me I didn't know existed.

When I feel his lips on the small of my back and his finger scraping against my prostate, I can't stand waiting any longer. "Make love to me, Adam. I need you. I need you so bad."

"And I need you, sweetheart." He climbs on top of me, the weight of his muscular body pressing me against the mattress.

I can feel the head of his cock against my anus.

"Ready?" he asks softly, feathering his lips against my ear.

Instead of answering with words, I fist the sheets, bite the pillow, and shift back into him, taking his cock into my ass. My flesh stretches beyond the imaginable. He's enormous and the shock rocks my entire body. But an instant later, I'm rocking my hips back and forth to take him deeper and deeper. He grabs my wrists and plunges into me again and again. Sensations explode inside me the deeper I take him. I feel electricity sparking vibrations throughout my body.

Every one of his thrusts that invades my ass claims more and more of me. I'm his. There's no holding back anything from Adam. Not anymore. This is the most intimate feeling I've ever experienced. I'm drowning in unbelievable pleasure and raw emotions. He loves me. And I…I love him.

Having him inside me is intense and pleasurable, too potent for words. I realize this is so much more than just sex. This is fiery and all-consuming. He's all that matters to me. My old life is vanishing, morphing into something new. The pleasure he's giving me impacts not just my body but also my whole heart. Invisible ties are binding me to him for tonight—and forever. He is the man I've needed my whole life.

Say it, Oliver.

I take a deep breath. I can't hold back my feelings any longer. "I love you, Adam. I love you so much."

"I love you, too." He kisses the back of my neck, rolls both of us onto our sides, keeping his dick seated deep inside me.

He reaches around me and grabs my cock, stroking me fast and furious, while continuing to thrust into my ass again and again.

I lift my leg to take more of him into my body. "Oh God. So close."

"Yes. Yes." He clamps down on my ear, his breathing primal and hot. He thrusts into me deep, and lets out a long groan. "Ahh."

My entire body stiffens as he continues fisting my cock. When I climax, everything inside me explodes. I can't breathe for a moment and my heart skips a beat. Once I'm able to gulp in some much needed oxygen, my heartbeats slow slightly and my breathing, though shaky, begins to soften.

We cuddle together, me in the front and Adam behind me. Time has no meaning when I'm in his arms.

I twist around to face him, gazing into his deep blue eyes. "I need to explain something to you."

He kisses me lightly. "I'm listening."

"When you told me you loved me the other night, I couldn't say it back. I'm sorry."

Again, his lips brush mine. "Nothing to be sorry about, baby. You told me you loved me tonight. That's all I needed to hear."

"God, you are too good for me."

"And you're too good for me."

I smile. "Sex has never been like this for me, sweetheart. Because of what happened to me before I met Malcolm, I always forced myself to turn off my emotions whenever I was with a man. It's how I survived. But you—"

"Me." He smiles.

"With you I can't turn off my emotions. In fact, with you the switch is always on 'high.'" I touch his face. "I love you. I've known it for some time now. I love you so much."

"And I love you." He smiles, kisses me again. "But I've also learned something tonight."

"What's that?"

"Swimming followed by sex makes me hungry. You got anything we could snack on in your kitchen?"

In a state of utter bliss, I press my lips to his. "How about ice cream? I could use some cooling off."

Chapter 22

Since I've lived in Dallas longer than Adam, I'm driving him and Mom to DFW Airport to get his grandfather. We're all nervous about how things might go once Adam tells his grandfather he's gay.

Adam sits in the backseat while Mom sits next to me in the passenger seat.

Mom.

I can't get over that she actually thinks of me as her son now. I actually think of her as Mom now, too. It's wonderful to have a loving, selfless mother in my life.

I keep glancing at Adam in the rearview mirror, wishing I could be the one to tell his grandfather. Adam must be playing every kind of scenario in his mind of how his grandfather might respond. No one knows how anyone will react when they share their truth with those they love. I certainly didn't.

"How are you doing back there?" I ask him.

"Not good. I'm worried how Granddad is going to take this news. I don't want to lose him, but I can't live a lie any longer." He reaches forward and squeezes my shoulder. "Especially since I've found you. I won't lie. I'm proud to be with you, Oliver. And as you so eloquently say, I will live in my truth."

Mom turns around and says to Adam, "Your Granddad is a good man. He'll understand. And even if he doesn't at first, he will in time. And you won't be alone when you tell him."

I nod. "That's right. Mom and I will be beside you."

"That wouldn't be fair to Granddad," he says. "I've been giving this a lot of thought. If the three of us jump out and I tell him I'm gay, that would be an ambush. I know you both wanted to be next to me when I give him the news, and I appreciate that more than you can know. But this is something I need to do on my own. I love him. He deserves his own private reaction. You understand?"

"Of course I understand," I tell him. "But if I see you getting upset, don't blame me for rushing out of the car."

"What Oliver said." Mom nods. "Me, too."

Adam smiles. "You sure neither of you served in the Marines before?"

"Semper Fi," Mom and I say in unison and the three of us laugh. It breaks the apprehension we are feeling for a brief moment.

I pass the airport's tollbooths and drive to Terminal A, where his grandfather's gate is.

When I pull up to the area where vehicles are allowed to load and unload passengers, Mom says, "I see him, Adam. He's standing right by the door."

"I see him, too."

"Which one is he?" I ask.

"The guy with the blue baseball cap," Adam tells me.

From what I can see, Adam's grandfather is about six foot tall and in great shape. He's clean shaven and his clothes are very neat.

I park the car by the curb.

Adam squeezes my shoulder again, leans over the seat and kisses Mom. "Wish me luck, you two."

He gets out and shuts the door.

Mom and I watch as Adam walks to his grandfather.

"Please let this go well," she says, grabbing my hand.

I brace myself, ready to run to Adam's side.

I feel my heart pounding as I watch them greet each other with a hug. "So far so good, Mom."

"It has to be good. It just has to be. Those two are crazy about each other. When Pop sees how happy Adam is now, I can't imagine him not accepting Adam for who he is."

"Adam is happy, isn't he?"

"Yes, Oliver. This is the first time I've seen him this happy since he lost his leg." She squeezes my hand. "And you are the reason why."

"I can't take any credit, but I'm happier than I've ever been, too."

We watch as Adam talks to his grandfather.

"I wish we could hear what they're saying to each other," Mom says. "I'm a nervous wreck."

"Am I seeing tears from your father-in-law?"

"I think so. My God, I've only seen him cry once at my husband's funeral."

"But are his tears a good thing or bad thing?"

"Damn it, I don't know." She's just as wound up as I am.

Another minute passes. And then another.

"How long do you think this will take, Oliver?"

"I haven't a clue. But Adam isn't talking anymore. It looks like he's waiting for your father-in-law to respond."

Adam and his grandfather silently face each other for what seems like an eternity but is actually only a few seconds.

"Say something, Pop. Don't just stand there."

When I see Adam's grandfather start shaking his head, I grab the door handle, but then I see the two embrace. I release the handle, breathing a sigh of relief.

"Oh, Oliver. Pop gets it. He understands."

We watch them walking to my car, pulling the suitcase behind them arm in arm and all smiles. I'm so thrilled that Adam's granddad seems to have responded perfectly to learning his grandson is gay.

Mom and I get out of the car and I open the trunk.

"Hey, Pop." She wraps her arms around the man.

"Hi, sweetheart." He turns and looks at me. "And you must be Oliver. Adam just told me so much about you, young man."

I extend my hand, but his grandfather ignores it, pulling me into a hug and patting me on the back.

"I can't thank you enough for helping Adam." He steps back, wiping his eyes. "He's happy, truly happy. Now I have two grand-sons, if you'll have me, Oliver?"

"Have you? I'm absolutely honored and proud that you want me in your family, sir."

"Son, call me 'Granddad.'"

"Okay, Granddad. I will." Taking his suitcase, I place it in my trunk. I'm overwhelmed how lucky I am. It all started with Adam moving into Unit A. I fell in love with him and he with me. And not only do I get to be with him, I get to have a new family.

We get back in my car—Mom and me in the front and Adam and Granddad in the back.

As I drive out of the airport and onto the freeway, Granddad says, "Adam, I have a pretty good idea why it's taken you this long to tell me you're gay. It was those horrible jokes my friends and I told each other in front of you, right?"

"That was part of it, yes, but so was 'Don't Ask, Don't Tell.'"

"I understand. The military was about as stupid as I was. But thank goodness they've gotten it right now. And so have I. Adam, those jokes were crass and hurtful. I should have known better. There's no excuse for my bad behavior. I'm sorry. Can you ever forgive me?"

"Yes. Granddad, that's all in the past now."

I see in the rearview Adam putting his arm around Granddad.

Change is hard and even impossible for some, like my parents. But for others, like Granddad, they embrace change, letting go of wrong thinking and bigotry.

Once we are back at Adam's condo, he hands each of us a beer, and we toast Granddad's arrival. Adam shows him around his place and Mom and I sit down on the sofa.

When they go up the stairs, I whisper to Mom, "I want to tell Granddad about my past. More than that even. He deserves to know. He blew me away when he asked me to be his grandson. I *need* to tell him."

"Yes, you do. We're all going to gather around to visit. When the opportunity arrives to tell him, you'll know it. But if not today, then tomorrow. Or the next day. There's no rush."

"Thanks, but I don't want to put it off too long." I smile and take a sip of beer. "Now that everything is out in the open with you and Adam, I don't want to ever hide that part of my life again. It helped make me who I am today. God, I feel like a weight has been lifted off of me."

"I feel the same way. I've been so worried about Adam every since he lost his leg. But you helped us to get to the real issue. No more secrets for any of us anymore." She kisses me lightly on the cheek. "I couldn't have asked for better men for my sons than you and Adam. You're both perfect. Absolutely perfect."

I laugh. "I don't know about that, Mom, but I do love our family and I love Adam with all my heart."

Adam and Granddad come down the stairs and join us in the living room.

"This is a terrific place." Granddad smiles at me. "And Adam told me you helped him get everything put together. Great job."

"Thanks." His praise makes me feel terrific.

"Did Adam ever tell you about his first fishing trip I took him on?"

"No, sir."

"Well, he was only four years old at the time and so excited. I crossed my fingers that he would catch a fish. I even planned on putting one I caught on his hook when he wasn't looking if he didn't. But he did catch his own fish. I had to hold onto him or it would have pulled him off the shore and into the river. He was yelling, 'Granddad, help. Granddad, help.' So I put my hand over his and helped him reel it in. That bass was almost as big as Adam was. Bigger than any I'd caught that entire season." Granddad smiles broadly. "When we got back to the house, Adam wanted to carry that fish up to the front door by himself to show his mom."

"I was proud of myself," Adam says with a big grin.

Mom turns to me. "We were proud of him, but you should have seen that fish. When I opened the door, it was in bad shape covered in dirt and gravel. That bass was too heavy for him to carry, so he had to drag it all the way to the door."

I envision an image of a smiling five-year-old Adam holding the bass with both his tiny hands. "What happened to the fish?"

"I cleaned it up," Granddad says. "And fileted it."

"And I cooked it," Mom adds.

Adam nods. "Best fish I've ever eaten."

She laughs. "I'm glad you caught that bass because until then you wouldn't eat even a bite of fish no matter how hard I tried to get you to."

"Me, too. I love fish now."

"That's a great story," I say. "Granddad, are there more stories you can tell me about Adam as a kid?"

He pats me on the back. "You bet there are, Oliver. I remember the time he was learning to drive and backed my truck into the side of my house."

Adam groans. "Not that story again."

"Oh yes, again." Granddad stands. "But I need a fresh beer. Anyone else?"

We all raise our hands, which makes us laugh.

"Another round coming right up."

The four of us talk for hours. Each story they share deepens my love for Adam and for them. This is how a real family, a loving family, is supposed to treat each other.

Granddad finishes another tale about Adam's teenage years and then turns to me. "We've been going on and on about Adam. How about you tell us something from your childhood, Oliver?"

I look at Mom. "I think this is the opportunity you were talking to me about earlier."

"I think so too." She reaches for my hand.

I turn back to Granddad. "My parents weren't like you and Mom. They were cold and distant. I don't remember hearing them laugh or saying they loved me."

I tell him about coming out to my father and mother, about the ranch, about how I arrived in Dallas, and about those horrific six months before being rescued by Malcolm.

When I finish my story, I see that Granddad and Mom have tears trickling down their cheeks.

Adam puts his arm around me. "What do you think of *my* hero, Granddad?"

"I wish…I wish…" Grandad's voice shakes. He looks straight at me. "I wish I could have been there for you, Oliver. But I promise you one thing, I will be there for you from now on."

I feel my eyes welling up. "And I will be there for you, Granddad." I share Malcolm's definition of what a real family is. "Blood isn't thicker than water, Granddad. Love is. That's what makes a real family."

Chapter 23

Everything is perfect for Martha and Sarah's wedding. The flowers. The music. The weather. The soft pink rug rolled out to designate an aisle between the chairs.

Waiting for the signal from Granddad inside my condo, I look out my window at the pool as he asks everyone to take their seats in the folding chairs facing Malcolm's tree. Granddad will be conducting the ceremony.

Adam stands next to me. He and I will be walking Martha and Sarah down the aisle. Candy is their maid of honor and Mom is their matron of honor.

When Martha and Sarah met Mom and Granddad, the four of them hit it off from the start. They asked Mom to stand up with them and Granddad to officiate, informing him that he could get ordained in less than twenty-four hours online. They both agreed and Granddad is asking everyone to call him 'Rev' now. I am a wreck, of course, because of the last minute changes, but that's my Martha and Sarah, always living on the edge.

Candy hands the blushing brides their matching bouquets, pale pink roses. Her doctor released her days ago. I'm so thrilled how fast she's recovering. I have no doubt she'll be ready for the trip to DC next month to meet the president. She is a former Marine after all.

"These are something old." Candy gives Martha and Sarah earrings. "I got them when I graduated from high school."

"Thank you, sweetheart." Sarah kisses her on the cheek.

Martha kisses her other cheek. "You're a doll."

Mom gives Martha and Sarah matching necklaces. "This is something new for you."

"I love them," Martha says. "Don't you, S?"

"I certainly do. Thanks, Kathy."

"And this is for borrowed." Candy puts a ring on Martha's right hand.

Mom also places another ring on Sarah's hand.

"And for blue, Candy and I got you these." Mom holds up two blue garters.

Smiling, Martha and Sarah slip them on.

"Oh God, I had no idea I would be this nervous." Martha looks incredible in the dress she and Mom selected for this special day— an off-white, V-neck, long-sleeved sheath. "Are you as nervous as I am, S?"

"Very nervous, M." Sarah is just as gorgeous in her dress—the same color as Martha's but with a round collar and high bodice with a full skirt—also chosen with Mom's help.

"I still think it's hysterical you call each other S and M," Mom says. "So does the Rev."

Martha grins and shakes her head. "Kathy, we've already told you about that."

"But Adam doesn't know, do you Adam?"

"No. Please tell me."

I send him and Mom a wink, realizing they're trying to get Martha and Sarah to relax.

"Martha and I were so naive when we met." Sarah smiles at the love of her life. "So very young. We started calling each other S and M without knowing what that actually meant to most people."

Adam chuckles. "I'm sorry. It's just so funny."

Martha and Sarah start laughing with him.

"It is funny," Martha says, gazing at her bride-to-be. "To us it has only meant 'Sarah' and 'Martha.' Nothing else. But every time we tell this story to someone new, we always burst into laughter."

Sarah nods. "When it was finally brought to our attention about that *other meaning*, you can't imagine how embarrassed we were."

Mom giggles. "Oh, yes we can."

"I can see Malcolm now cracking up like it was yesterday, though it was several decades ago when he told S and me." Martha lowers her voice and imitates Malcolm. "Girls, S and M means sadomasochism.' And then I asked him, 'Is that a name of a company or something?'"

We bust out laughing.

Mom grabs the brides' hands. "I can see why you didn't want to follow the tradition of not seeing each other on the most special day of your lives."

"Who in the world came up with such a silly idea any way?" Martha leans over and gives Sarah a tender kiss. "I don't want to be with anyone more than I want to be with Sarah."

"Same here, M."

I hear Red Shimmer start playing Mendelssohn's "Wedding March," and see Granddad give the signal.

I look at Martha and Sarah. "Ready?"

They nod, and I open my door.

Candy goes down the aisle first, followed by Mom.

Martha takes my arm and Sarah takes Adam's, and we walk down the aisle to where Granddad is waiting for us. In the chairs are the people who are part of our little family. Lashaya and Hayden, sit together. She made the wedding cake and he set up the chairs. Trace and Jackson are hosting the reception at their place after the service. Eli and Jaris bought the food and Tony got the liquor.

Once Martha and Sarah are in their places in front of Granddad, we move to our positions—Mom and Candy to one side of the brides and me on the other. Adam will join me after he sings.

He walks over to Josh, Chad, and Franki. Taking a microphone, he begins singing a love song.

I'm filled with pride. That's *my* Marine singing. God, I'm so in love with him.

Adam finishes and steps next to me.

"You did great," I whisper.

He winks at me.

"We are gathered here to witness a momentous occasion, the marriage of Martha Rivers and Sarah Barnett," Granddad says. "This is just one stop on a journey of love they began when they were very young. Ladies, please take each other's hand."

The two beautiful brides let go of our arms and reach for each other.

"Martha and Sarah, you joined together as one long ago. Back then our government didn't recognize the promises you made to each other. But now we are here to celebrate the public expression of your unbreakable commitment. I understand that you wrote your own vows. Martha, we'll begin with you."

Martha gazes into Sarah's eyes. "S, we've been through so much together. Laughter and tears. Up and downs. Sickness and health. Better and worse. This is old hat to us, isn't it? I fell in love with a curvy blonde soprano. But I had no idea that my love for you would keep growing and growing. Nothing has really changed for us, except our dream finally came true. We're about to be legal. I promise to do my best to always turn off the shower so you don't get your head soaked when you turn on the water."

Everyone laughs.

"And I promise to do my best to not flush the toilet when you're taking a shower."

Sarah smiles and shakes her head.

"And I promise to do my best to rinse the dishes before I put them in the dishwasher."

"M, I'm getting more out of this wedding than I thought," Sarah says, and we all roar.

"But most of all, S, I promise to never stop loving you, not that that's even possible." Martha leans forward and kisses Sarah.

Granddad chuckles. "Aren't you supposed to wait for the minister to give you permission to do that?"

Martha grins and holds up her fists. "Try to stop me, Rev."

"I wouldn't dare," Granddad says.

More laughter follows.

This wedding is perfect for her and Sarah—very non-traditional and fun, just like them.

Sarah pulls Martha's fists down. "Now, M. You know you're my heart. So you don't have to make all those crazy promises. I've been with you all these years, getting my hair soaked when I turn on the bathtub's faucet, getting scalded when you flush the toilet when I'm in the shower, and getting to pull the dirty dishes out of the dishwasher that you forgot to rinse. I've never left and I don't ever intend to. What you did forget to say was all the sleep you lost when I was in the hospital. You were by my side, night after night. And what about the time our dog Lilly died. I was so brokenhearted I couldn't think. You planned the most beautiful funeral and then took me on a cruise so my heart would start healing. That's just a couple of things you've done for me from a very long list. You're my rock, M. You always have been. You know I love you and I always will. And I know you love me and always will. There's nothing new to say here today that we haven't said to each other thousands of times. You're mine. I'm yours. That's how it is, how it's always been." She looks at Granddad and winks. "May I kiss my bride, Rev?"

He smiles. "Be my guest."

Sarah plants a whopper of a kiss on Martha and everyone cheers.

As Martha and Sarah exchange rings, I glance at Adam, *my* Marine. I'm lucky to have him in my life.

"By the power vested in me by the state of Texas and supported by the Constitution of the United States of America, it gives this old Marine and now reverend the great honor to pronounce you, Martha Rivers and you, Sarah Barnett legally married."

Everyone comes to their feet and applauds.

Granddad continues, "Now, or should I say 'again,' you may kiss each other."

Martha and Sarah kiss and everyone cheers once again.

"Now let's party," the newlyweds shout in unison.

As they and the rest of the wedding guests walk toward Trace and Jackson's place, Adam grabs my arm and we stop under Malcolm's tree. We kiss each other tenderly.

"One day we'll be standing where they were, Oliver, professing our love to each other with Granddad officiating right here in the courtyard of Mockingbird Place."

"I can't wait."

Adam reaches in his coat pocket and pulls out a key. "I'd like you to move back into Unit A. It was your home and now it can be *our* home."

"Oh my God, yes." I take the key and kiss him.

He's my life, my love, my forever. *He's the Marine of my dreams.*

Chapter 24

dam - *two months later*

TODAY IS OUR YARD SALE.

Oliver moved in with me weeks ago. We went through his stuff and mine and picked out what we wanted to keep. I thought Unit A looked great before. But now that we have put our things together and Oliver has worked his magic, our place could be featured on HGTV.

We're clearing out his old apartment, Unit D, so that it can be rented. When our neighbors heard we were having a yard sale with the proceeds going to the Lifeline Foundation, they not only donated more items but also insisted on helping us. Mockingbird Place's courtyard was packed with furniture, clothes, dishes, tools, and more. Now that the sale is almost over, there are just a few items remaining.

Oliver is still keeping us on task. He put me in charge of

handling the money. We're already way over what we thought we would bring in. Our friends are following Oliver's orders to the letter. They are manning the tables and reading from the information cards he made for every item, including the things marked for less than a dollar. My guy gives a new meaning to the word "organized."

Lashaya is at the table closest to mine. We just learned she's pregnant and everyone is thrilled, especially Hayden, who is making sure she doesn't over do it today.

Candy is in charge of the furniture we're selling. Many of today's customers recognize Candy, Oliver, and me from the news of our meeting with the president and First Lady in DC. Oliver tried to get out of going but Candy and I were able to convince him in the end. The president was impressed with what Oliver had to say about homeless teenagers. He even gave him some names of potential donors for the Lifeline Foundation.

Last week, Franki moved away from Mockingbird Place to live with Candy in her home. Oliver suggested they move into his old place, but they decided Candy's apartment would be better since it is so much larger. They don't live far. Plus, we still get to see them on campus. Oliver and I and everyone else are so happy for them. Next to Malcolm's tree, Franki, Josh, and Chad are performing. Oliver's idea again. He thought live music would attract more people to the sale. He was right.

"I can let you have the entire box of DVDs for fifty dollars," Jackson tells the man at his table. Jackson and I are in a class together. Accounting 101. Getting to study with him has been great. We both aced our last test.

Tony is carrying some boxes to the parking lot for a woman who has bought several things. Last week, Oliver and I went to one of Tony's fights, which he won. That guy is a beast.

Jaris and Eli weren't able to make the yard sale. They both have shifts to work, but they donated items and money. They rarely get to do anything with us, but when they do they are so much fun to be around.

As the sale winds down, Trace has a couple at his table and waves Martha and Sarah over. The young woman looks like she's about to have her baby any day. The man? Handsome guy. It's obvious he's a cowboy with his Stetson hat, Levi jeans, big belt buckle, and western boots.

"This is Luke and Ava," Trace tells Martha and Sarah. "They're interested in seeing Unit E and Oliver's place, too."

"We'd love to show them to you," Sarah says to the couple. "But Unit E is ready today. Unit D won't be available until next Sunday."

Oliver and I are going to paint his old apartment this week.

"Thank you so much." Luke puts his arm around Ava. It's obvious how much they care about one another. "We've heard good things about Mockingbird Place."

As Martha and Sarah lead Luke and Ava into Unit E, the last shopper leaves, and we begin boxing up the few remaining items that didn't sell, which will be donated to charity.

Oliver walks up to me and gives me a kiss. "Hey, sweetheart."

"Hi, baby. You did such an incredible job putting this together. I haven't finished counting the money yet but I know we've made at least four grand."

"Four grand? That's fantastic." He kisses me again. "I love you."

"I love you, too."

"Adam, did you see the cowboy and his pregnant wife?"

"Yes I did, sweetheart."

"I think those two might fit in perfectly with our little family."

I pull him into my arms. "Just like you and I fit together."

"Like biscuits and gravy." He smiles. *God, how I love his smile.*

"Or peanut butter and jelly," I add.

"Or steak and a baked potato." Oliver laughs. "I guess we're both hungry, honey."

"Starving."

"I think we should go into our place and fix some sandwiches for us and everyone else."

"I like that idea very much. We can leave the rest of the cleanup until after our appetites…are sated."

The End

READ on for an excerpt for the next book in the Mockingbird Place series.

Excerpt

The Cowboy in Unit E

The good news is the most gorgeous cowboy I've ever seen is moving in next door to me.

The bad news? He's not alone.

Hanging on his arm is a very pregnant woman.

Are they a couple? It sure looks like they are.

So not only is he not gay, but he also has a girlfriend, or a wife, or whatever.

Just my luck.

Excerpt:

Out of the corner of my eye through the window I see one of my new neighbors walking up the sidewalk. Ava Stone is pregnant and carrying a box. In her current condition I wonder if she should be lifting heavy things.

Ava and her good-looking cowboy, Luke Wagner, are moving into the apartment next to Jackson's and mine. Unit E has remained empty for quite some time. Until now. I'm glad it's finally going to be occupied and hope the new couple will be good neighbors.

The three owners of Mockingbird Place are Oliver, Martha and Sarah. They are good friends. Jackson and I are so happy for Oliver. He and Adam, our resident former-Marine, fell in love and are living in Unit A. Oliver is more of a silent partner since he is still in college. So Martha and Sarah manage Mockingbird Place. But all three are picky about who they rent to, wanting to make sure whoever moves in are people that will become part of our community.

I've been here for two years. This 10-unit 1950s Mediterranean complex is not just where I live but also is my home. Most of the residents are gay and lesbian college students like Jackson and me. I wonder if our new neighbors will be able to fit in.

I see Ava collapse. A blast of electricity shoots through my body, and I toss my brushes aside and rush out my door.

"Ava. Ava." I lift her head off the ground and start shouting for her boyfriend. "Luke. Get out here. Ava has passed out." *Where the hell is he?*

Her eyes open. "What happened?"

"You must have passed out and fell."

"Oh God." Ava rubs her hands over her belly. "I think the baby is okay."

"Where's Luke?"

Before she can answer, I see him running up the sidewalk.

He kneels down next to me and shoves a sack of burgers in my chest. "My God, Ava, what happened? Are you okay?"

"I'm fine. I'm fine. Everything is fine."

"I'm not so sure about that," I say. "She passed out."

She shakes her head. "You didn't have to tell on me, mister…?"

"Trace Cotton, your next door neighbor." I set the sack to the side and Luke and I help her up into a sitting position.

"Thanks for your help, Trace, but I need to get her to the hospital." Luke is clearly in a protective, possessive state of mind. I can't blame him. This cowboy is one of the good guys.

Ava nods anxiously. "Yes. I want to make sure the baby is okay."

"Let me take you." I tell them, picking up the burgers. "I know the quickest route to the hospital."

"Perfect. You drive and I'll take care of her."

Luke lifts her up off the ground.

"I can walk, Luke," she says.

"Not until we get the doctor's okay."

I lead them to my car. Luke gets in the back with Ava. I get behind the wheel, realizing I'm still holding onto the sack of burgers. I place them in the passenger seat and start the engine. I drive to the hospital as fast as I can.

When we get to the hospital, I let them out in front of the emergency room doors. Despite her objections, Luke carries Ava inside.

I park the car and send a text to Jackson, who is still in class, about what is going on. I walk into the waiting room just as a nurse is leading Ava and Luke through a set of double doors.

Anticipating that it might be a little while before they come back out, I take a seat. Even though I only just met Ava and Jackson, they seem like a perfect couple. I hope Ava and their baby are okay.

My phone buzzes.

It's a text from Jackson. *Just got out of class. Any word yet about our new neighbor?*

Luke just carried Ava into the ER. I'll let you know when we get word from the doctor.

If you need me for any reason let me know.

I can always count on Jackson. *I've got this covered for now. If something changes I'll call you. Otherwise I'll see you at home.*

Later.

My stomach growls. I forgot to eat. Realizing Luke's meal will go bad, I decide to go back to my car and get his sack of burgers. After we finish here, I'll buy him and Ava fresh ones.

I step up to the nurses' station.

"May I help you?" the woman behind the desk asks.

"I came in with the couple who just went to the back—the cowboy and pregnant lady. I need to run to my car to get something. If they come out would you let them know I'll be right back?"

"Of course, but you have plenty of time I'm sure."

"Thank you." I walk to my car and open my door.

My cell buzzes again. This time it's a phone call—from Martha. I grab the sack and answer the call. "Hey, Martha."

"I just got a text from Jackson about Ava," Martha says in a tone full of concern. "S found the box on the sidewalk she dropped when she passed out. Do you know how she's doing?"

"No word yet but we haven't been here very long." I'm not surprised Jackson sent her a text. One thing about Mockingbird Place you can always count on is—*we take care of each other*. Sometimes that can appear like we are into each other's business a little too much, but whatever is done comes out of love, especially with Martha and Sarah.

"What can S and I do to help?"

I walk back into the waiting room and sit in the same chair. "We left so fast I know I didn't lock my door and they didn't either.

"S and I already took their box back inside Unit E and locked their door. I'll lock your door when we get off the phone. You don't worry about a thing here. Just take care of our new friends, Trace."

"I'll do my best."

We say goodbye.

My stomach growls again, this time more demanding than before. I walk to the soda machine and buy a Coke.

Back in my seat, I look at the bag and see, for the first time since we were too busy taking care of Ava earlier, that Luke's meal is from Aunt Connie's Burger Palace, which is located across the street from Mockingbird Place. I pull out one of the two cheeseburgers. I know it's a cheeseburger because it is wrapped in yellow paper. I leave the fries. There's no saving them. They're cold and limp.

I take a bite. Better if it was warmer, but not too bad. My stomach is just grateful. After I finish the burger, I look at the time on my phone. Luke and Ava have been back there for at least an hour. God, I hope she and the baby are okay.

Fifteen minutes later, Luke comes through the double doors and back into the waiting room.

Smiling, Luke holds up both his thumbs and walks over to me. He sits down and places his hand on top of mine. That's unusual, especially for a cowboy whose pregnant girlfriend is expecting their first baby.

"Trace, Ava and the baby are fine."

"I'm so glad." I leave my hand under his, wishing he were gay. "Honestly, I was getting worried because you were back there so long."

"That's because they were doing an ultrasound as well as checking her." His eyes light up. "You should see the little cowboy. Mick is going to be a big one."

"If he's anything like you, he will be. You've got to be at least six foot."

"Six-one, just like my brother. Everyone is pretty tall in my family." He leans back and removes his hand from mine.

I instantly miss his touch. Am I crazy? He's not available or even gay. Maybe he is just the touchy-feely type.

Luke picks up the sack from the table. "You and I are about the same height, aren't we?"

"I'm six foot. I ate one of your burgers, but I'll pay you back."

"There's no way you'll pay us back, Trace. I'm so grateful you brought us to the hospital. I'm especially thankful you were there when she first passed out. I don't what I would have done without you."

"That reminds me." I pull out my phone. "I need to let Jackson and Martha know that Ava and the baby are fine." As I fire off a text to Jackson and Martha, I tell Luke that Martha and Sarah took the box Ava dropped into their apartment and locked their door.

"Jackson is your boyfriend, right? The guy you live with?"

"Nope. We're just good friends."

"Oh. I thought you were gay."

I laugh. "I am gay and proud of it."

Luke nods. "I know that's right."

"I'm really not trying to be an asshole about it, but I *am* proud of who I am."

"You're absolutely right. We should be proud of who were are, Trace."

"Thanks for your understanding, Luke."

195

A nurse comes out from the back with Ava in a wheelchair.

Ava points at us. "There are my two knights in shinning armor."

We stand and walk over to her and the nurse.

"Can you bring your car around?" the nurse asks us.

"Certainly. I'll be right back." As I walk to my car, I glance at the hand that Luke touched. Why can't I find a gay guy like him? Good-looking and so kind.

About the Author

Lee Swift, who writes under several pen names including Kris Cook, creates novels, short stories, screenplays and more.

With an unquenchable thirst to experience all his life journey has to offer, Lee and hubby love travel but still call Dallas, Texas home.

Also by Lee Swift

Novels

Morvicti Blood *(Supernatural Thriller)*

Cupid's Arrow *(Gay Fantasy Romance)*

Three to Play *(Menage MMF Romance)*

(All series listed in best reading order)

Mockingbird Place

(Gay Romance Series)

The Marine in Unit A

The Cowboy in Unit E

The Fireman in Unit C

The Doctor in Unit H

The Fighter in Unit J

Holiday Beaus (Novella)

The Musician in Unit G

The Cop in Unit B

Wolf Pack

(Menage MFM Romance Trilogy)

Secret Cravings

Primal Desires

Delicious Hunger

Eternal Trio Series

(Gay Menage Fantasy Romance)

Levi's Rogues

Perfection

Writing with Lana Lynn

(Thrillers)

Lexi's Protector *(Men Without A Cause)*

Liz's Guardian *(Men Without A Cause)*

Secret Diary Series as Kris Cook

(Erotic Straight BDSM Trilogy)

Mia's Spanking Diary

Misty's Bondage Diary

Lea's Ménage Diary

Made in the USA
Middletown, DE
01 May 2021